Battenberg & Banter

(Book 1)

'Let's Go Blogging'

By
E M Taylor

About the Author

Elaine Taylor was born in Oldham, Lancashire and lived there until 1998 when she moved to Cornwall. After a successful career in Housing spanning over 22 years she was made redundant in 2014, following this Elaine worked for 12 months as a Head Housekeeper before obtaining her current position of General Services Assistant in a local hospital. Encouraged by a friend, Elaine started writing short stories in 2016 and in 2017 set up a Facebook Blog page 'Battenberg & Banter', which goes from strength to strength. Elaine enjoys travel and often disappears in her Campervan 'Trixie'. Having moved house twenty three times in her life she's a dab hand at decluttering and removals, although constantly mutters 'never again'. She has two sons, one daughter and two adorable Granddaughters Sienna Grace and Maisie Dorothy.

To, Gillian
Follow your dreams
E.m Taylor.

Copyright © 2018 E M Taylor
All rights reserved.
ISBN-13: 978-1726203296
Published by Createspace, Amazon
Design: Book cover by -
SelfPubBookCovers.com/3rustedspoons

Dedication

This book is dedicated to my parents Dorothy Taylor (deceased) and my dad William Edward Taylor a flat capped, hard working man from Oldham in Lancashire who enjoys fishing, a game of snooker, a packet of cigarettes and a pint at his local pub. If having a sense of humour is genetic, then 'Thank you dad', I inherited it from you.

I'd also like to mention my Great Auntie Annie who was a big part of my life from an early age until she died at the age of 92. She was a real character, had the longest, droopiest boobs I've ever seen, deaf as a post and made incessant farting noises, but couldn't hear them. She had a never ending drawer of chocolate bars, sucked Uncle Joes mint balls and had a 'teaspoon' of brandy in her tea every morning, for medicinal purposes only (her measuring was not very good). She could carry 20llb of potatoes back from the market and made the best strawberry and gooseberry pie you'll ever taste.

Humour is –

'Chewing gum for the brain' Luke Meader, Oxford, UK – Winner of Battenberg & Banter's Competition

'Good for your chuckle muscles' Margaret Parnell

'Contagious' Ken Messier

'Not funny if you haven't got a sense of it' Suzie Jones

'The remedy to cure sad souls' Alice Clover

' Every day spent with a toddler! I wish we could see the world through their eyes' Laura Braithwaie

'A tad funny' Karen Taylor

'Working with you' Nikki Garvey

'Helpful' Frankie Delson

'A feeling everyone wants to get from people' Okpanige Emmanuel Christian

'The icing that can make even the driest of cakes edible' Darren Walker

'Quite a laugh' Allison Senior

'Being able to laugh at yourself through the good and the bad' John Taylor

'The best medicine' Shelly Brierley'

'If laughter is the best medicine, let this book be the pill you want to swallow. Take a look inside this humorous collection of blogs about everyday life, from biscuit dunking, being single, menopause, dogging, to our John's shed, it's all in here. Recognise yourself amongst the chaos and laugh it off. Put your helmet on and get ready for the roller coaster of life' – E M Taylor

WARNING – ' Laughing for 15 minutes can burn off 40 calories'. This book may cause weight loss

Dear Reader

You're probably wondering what this books all about and whether it was worth giving up the huge bag of donuts, fizzy drink and six first class stamps you were going to buy, one of which you needed to put on a birthday card, which someone's not getting now. I can't promise to live up to that expectation, especially if the donuts were going to be dipped in cinnamon and sugar, however I will try my best and hope that by the time you've finished reading you're not looking for the dustbin. If you are, please save the planet and recycle the paper.

I apologise profusely in advance for any grammatical errors which I can assure you were added for the purpose of seeing how closely you are reading each page. I'm also posting a disclaimer here to cover my own ars*.

Disclaimer – If you think you recognise yourself, all my characters are fictional, aren't they S from Padstow (wink), except for my sister who is unfortunately real (joke). You should also note that I have no money so your lawsuit would be pointless.

The book serves two purposes, one being to promote laughter and give you the feel good factor and the second is to help with any diet you may be on because apparently laughing for fifteen minutes burns off forty calories, so be warned this book may cause weight loss.

I hope you enjoy reading it

Contents

Adjusting To Life As A Singleton 1

Whose Calling The Shots 5

Water, Babybels & Cherries 9

The Thong Answer 15

Pamper Me Not 19

Willy's & Rainbows 22

The Hospital Patient 25

Dog Meat Sandwiches And Life's A Bed Of Roses 30

To Do Or Not To Do? 34

Am I Menopausal? 39

Where There's A Blame 43

Exercise A Bad Thing Or Not? 46

Cucumber Sandwiches Or All You Can Eat? 50

Auntie Sarah's Birthday Party 54

Digital Diva 59

Hotels 'At Your Service' 62

Our John's Shed 68

It's A Mystery	73
Tenerife Here We Come!	77
Three Camels, A Volcano, And Slippers	82
It's Just Annoying	88
'Let's Go Dogging'	92
A Tale Of Biscuit Dunking	98
Black Friday Bargains Or Not?	103
Holidays Are Coming…	107
The Office Christmas Party	111
Knock, Knock, Knocking…	115
Peed Off And Seagulls	120
Jeff The Stand-In Best Man	124
Morning As Broken	127
Once Upon A Time	131
Thank You	133
References	134

Adjusting To Life as A Singleton

I wasn't really expecting to be on my own in my fifties, it just sort of happened. It's a bit like when you lose a slipper. The pair has been together for so long, which makes it hard to walk without the matching one, but you knew it had to go. It had become threadbare, restricted your walking and no longer matches as it once did. The refuse collection was on Tuesday, so on Monday night you decided to bin it, and once that slipper went through the crusher, there was no retrieving it.

It's strange at first being on your own. Like, when the post lands on your doormat, and you see the joint names. After a few moments, you glance sideways, before deciding whether to put it in the 'His' or 'Hers' piles. Bills, of course, are going on the right slipper pile. I say right because he was always right - Mr Right.

Once you've argued over who's having the bed, the table, the sofa and you have boxed up the cat ornament for him that his Aunt gave you and you never liked anyway, it's a fight for custody of the pets. I could have fought for custody and put serious thought into it at the time but, realistically, I'm always at work.

He walked and fed the dogs and if I'm sincere, I didn't like picking up steaming hot dog poo, only because, he would always buy the cheapest dog poo bags he could find when shopping, which always split allowing warm excrement to go on my fingers. It happened once in the park and the poor dog almost freaked out while I was jumping about looking for something to wipe my hand on, my memory often recalls poo#.

Facts about divorce – In the UK more than 13,000 women aged 55 and above divorced in 2016, while for men the figure was 19,454 - both double-digit percentage rises in rates per married population and raw numbers compared to 2015

Shopping is another area, where life is never the same again. You wander into the supermarket, put your coin in the huge trolley, before looking at your sad little list and replace it with a basket. Venturing down each aisle, you reach the ready meal for one section, a quick check over your shoulder to make sure no one is looking, and you put the meal in your basket. It's important to avoid eye contact in this section as I have heard that there have been occurrences of phone number exchanging over the ratatouille, which reminds me of the antics of a friend. At the local supermarket, she waits until someone leaves their trolley and then, moves it, usually a couple of aisles away and watches, as they search for it frantically. Another one of her set pieces involves an extra item of shopping, a conveyor belt and a stranger. When the protests and denials, regarding knowledge of said item begin (worse, if another assistant has to be called for), there's one person in the queue smiling, knowingly. Now, it might be my age but I was quite amused by this, and although I haven't done the deed myself, I'm beginning to feel I might do something similar, in the not too distant future. The friend will remain anonymous, for her own safety, concerning past, present and future victims.

■ Bedtime is bliss, no fighting over the duvet; you can go to bed in anything, PJ's, full combat gear, or completely naked. You don't have to pretend to be enjoying 'the moment', faking a period or bringing out the headache tablets and screaming the words PMT at him, while re-enacting scenes from The Omen.

I'm not saying it's all great, but being a Singleton presents more options, as you've already escaped (big tick!) it can be quite exciting to find someone new (even bigger tick!).

It's important to be selective with potential partners, because despite all the creams on the market, ones that firm and tone and bronze and lighten, (believe me) I've tried them all, nature gets you in the end. A partner who spends more time, money and effort on his looks than you do, is going to have a hard time accepting the demise of his own body, let alone yours.

Tip: - Share your body parts wisely.

Finally, for those who drink, alcohol is **not** your friend. Let's face it you don't want to wake up, find someone's nicked half the duvet, moved their stuff in and you can't remember his name…worse still, he's brought his slippers.

Who's calling the shots

I wanted to share with you the free entertainment, lets call it the local talent (I use this term loosely) that passes my house every Friday night. I say Friday, but it could be any night, Friday, Saturday, bank holiday, BBQ, family gathering, any night were copious amounts of alcohol hit the back of the throat and suddenly from nowhere a character appears, a bit like Jeckyl & Hyde. If you're with them, you'll know what I mean. Sometimes, the transition involves the removal of clothing and displaying of body parts, better left covered up at any time. For others, it's the discovery of a new voice, suddenly they see the world completely differently through their beer goggles. I can hear the clip-clop of a stiletto tapping down the pavement. Occasionally, they swerve into the road, at which point the shoes are off and barefoot is then the way to go... I prefer not to disclose my location, let's just say I'm strategically placed for front row seats, tickets not required and usually get my popcorn ready for the start about 0.30am onwards. I wouldn't say I was curtain twitching; I don't have to be near the window or curtains to hear the 'pubs out' performance. In fact, my duvet provides additional comfort during the interval, this is the period after the 'pubs out' people have gone home and the 'nightclubs' out characters emerge from the wings resplendent in their finery...

This Friday's performance was mild in comparison to some nights. It is however a truly compelling viewing. What better the secret life of others at your fingertips and when the beer goggles are on the truth, feelings and secrets emerge. Thoughts vocalise and trip off the tongue like a rocket going to the moon at the speed of light and beyond, actions of Oscar Performance standards. Sometimes, I want to clap but restrain myself from doing so. I fear they may stop their performance; the character will disappear and they will become just a mundane passer-by walking home. Alternatively, they may smash my window or pee up my garden wall, none of which are required.

So, Forest Gump; Yes, you the man who loudly and proudly declared three times while walking up the road he wanted to be Forest Gump all I can say is... Really? Mama always said 'Life was like a box of chocolates, you never know what you're gonna get.' So, lets unwrap you shall we...Your definitely not a Turkish delight, maybe a caramel barrel or some sort of nut....Anyway, whatever floats your boat. I'm sure if you Google it (yes Google is our friend) some Amateur Operatic Dramatic Society will be looking for their very own Forest Gump. Good Luck with that one.

I'll mention only two more characters. The first one, let's called him Ivor. He decided to do a three-point turn in the middle of the road to pick up his hoody friend. Ivor then screams, 'Get your head down', now this could be taken in more than one way, but we'll assume and because it's before the 9 pm watershed at the moment, that this was not a sexual innuendo. This would have been difficult, with the speed at which the car was moving and the position on 2 wheels it was angled at, as it screeched to a halt. Further up the road, it appears Ivor likes a good horn honking.

Finally, these are in no particular order. I'm not sure what to call this one, but his friend (maybe ex-friend) now, prefers to shout, 'You're a little prick'. This could be due to the size of his manhood for which solutions could be sought, penis enhancement etc.. But I felt on this occasion, he was indeed a little prick. He doesn't need a name, because this is one person that we all we know.

You'll notice that no females were present. This is not because they all went home with their halos intact, far from it.

No humans were hurt during tonight's performance (a few came close due to passing cars) I thank Forest Gump, Ivor & Little Prick for taking part this week.

Elaine signs off from secret location X

***Did you know?** According to the Guinness Book of world records the largest box of chocolates is a Thorntons Moments box weighing 1,690 kg (3,725 lbs.). It was produced by Thorntons and Russell Beck Studios and weighed in Bethnal Green, London, UK, on 2 April 2008.*

The box was 5040 mm (16 ft 6 in) long, 3420 mm (11 ft 2 in) wide and 1000 mm (3 ft 3 1/2 in) deep.

Water, Babybels & Cherries

■ I suppose you're wondering why the title. I decided to take the above items into work for my mid-morning break. Now, I like to think of myself as a very organised person and for anyone, who knows me well, know that I can, having had much practice pack up my entire house ready to move in approximately 2 hours. This ability to pack up quick is not because I am being chased for money or criminal activity (although occasional deviant thoughts often cross my mind). It is, purely that I do not like clutter in my house. In my mind, if it's not useful, it's not staying. I can see you looking around, and glancing now at your partner and thinking. I always wanted to be a rebel, but the closest I got to it, was having my ears pierced at 16. My mother nearly freaked out when I walked through the front door showing off my pierced ears and diamond studs. Her words, ringing in my ears, 'if God had wanted us to have holes in our ears, he would have given them to us', along with the usual 'wait till your father gets home'. Surprisingly, she never went to church except for the usual births, marriages and deaths, but somehow God was always on her side, except for the day I told her I was pregnant (I'd only just turned eighteen). On that day, God failed to catch her, after she passed out at the news of her infidel daughter. If you're wondering about her welfare, she was perfectly ok, after the initial shock and swift usage of smelling salts, by a neighbour, whom I could see was itching to get out of the door. This was MAJOR gossip in the small town I lived in. Gossip travels fast, the church choir visited me the following week, thanking me for my regular attendance in the choir and gave me a goodbye card and lovely bouquet of flowers, accompanied with a message about how much they'd miss me. It was a bit strange at the time because I hadn't said I was leaving. Looking back, they obviously thought my halo had slipped too far and I no longer made choir material. I never really did with a voice like mine I was only there to make numbers up and certainly wouldn't make the X Factor.

A bottle of water is essential at the hospital where I work, as it gets so hot. Drinking water can mean only one thing. I need the toilet, and depending on where you are, it can be a little inconvenient. I tend to plan any days out now, to ensure I am aware of the location of the nearest toilet, as my bladder is like a separate entity. It speaks to me regularly and, sometimes, without warning. Morning's, I get up and go to the toilet; have breakfast and go to the toilet; go to work and well, you know the rest. Often, it's just psychological and a mere dribble emerges, or nothing at all. When that happens, I sit there and urge myself to deliver, resorting to the tried-and-tested mantra: Come on, you know you want to. My toilet habits have become so noticeable, that my male stud of a work colleague, before a coffee break says to me: "I'll make the coffee because you'll want the toilet". I remember a night out, years ago, when I had to walk home, due to no taxi's being available. It was about 2 am and I desperately needed a wee. It was extremely dark and with no toilet facilities in sight, then I decided to go behind the blind centre. I knew this was a safe place to go, as it was, in actual fact, a centre for blind people and not a company that made blinds. I knew I had to be quick, having drunk several glasses of cider, so I ran like a whippet around the back. I saw a small wall, directly in front of me and thought, ideal it'll be dark behind there and no one will see me. What I didn't know (but found out very quickly), was that behind the wall, was a huge drop and, as I threw my leg over, let's just say my childbearing years were almost over, before they began. There are now devices that make it easy for women to wee anywhere, apparently. Take the Shewee™, for instance. You can splash out a little more (excuse the pun) for the Shewee™ Extreme, which comes with a carry case and extension tube. It doesn't say how long the tube is, but I'm sure it'll fit in the boot of most big cars (you could always get a trailer, if not). I'm still not sure how easy, or discreet, these are to use outside but, if anyone sees me frantically fiddling with my clothing, below the waist and in a public place, you'll know that I'm trying one out. If anyone's tried one, please let me know how you got on with it, and does the shake and repel liquid work? According to their advert, it does, and I wouldn't like to put it back into my handbag otherwise.

I love cherries.... I'm in the local petrol station looking around and this had to be the smallest punnet of cherries I had ever seen, at £1.75. I was, originally, buying nectarines, until I saw the flash of an orange discount sticker, out of the corner of my eye, being slapped across the top of the punnet and there it was: 44p... bargain! Even if I didn't like them, I'd probably have bought them, just so I could say: "Guess what? I just saved £1.31", to my daughter, whom I can declare has become a savvy shopper just like me.

Babybels... Having eaten them (and despite the fact I still can't decide if they actually taste of anything), I was wondering what I could do with the red wax wrapper. It has far more uses than you realise. You can make candles out of it and false eyeballs. Sculptures even. My talented friend tried this, while we were sitting at a picnic bench. I must say that his wax body parts were breath-taking. After a little playing around, I found that there was another, legitimate, use for the red stuff. I laughed at the idea of using it, in an emergency, as dental wax. I thought it was a pretty stupid idea until part of my filling fell out and I had to use my friends moulded body parts to fill the cavity in my mouth. I arrived at the dentist, with a red wax penis in my mouth - which was not how I had envisaged my day would turn out, however... the dentist let me take it home with me, after the procedure.

The moral of this story is not to waste anything and to consider whether it has a use, elsewhere. Unfortunately, it's going to take about 4 hours to pack up my house, as I've developed a love of Babybels and I'm becoming quite the wax sculptor.

The Thong Answer

I really don't want anyone to miss out, so I'm making you all aware of a couple of events that happen in January every year. The first is National Hat Day so time to get digging in your wardrobe and pull out your old beanie, rain hat or whatever.

In Ancient Greece and Rome when a slave was freed, they were often given a Phrygian cap that served as a symbol of their freedom. I personally love hats, but if you don't normally wear a hat, why not wear one just for the day. If someone you know notices and mentions it, act surprised and say, 'Did you not know it was National Hat Day today'. Have you ever been shopping for hats? I have, although only usually for weddings, which seem to be disappearing fast, and the occasional Christening, unless you count the woolly winter hats. I think it's quite therapeutic, being stood there in front of the mirror, doing a quick swop every 20 seconds, then the obligatory selfie and you always try on the, 'I wouldn't be seen dead in that one' hat, only to hear the assistant remark behind you, oh that looks lovely on you.

The second is National Hugging Day. I know not everyone's tactile, but now's your chance to change it, or at least for a day. Perhaps you've had your eye on someone, well time to grab the bull by the horns and give him or her a hug. It might be an idea to let them know why you're doing it, as you throw your arms around them and it's probably not designed for complete strangers, although you could brighten someone's day.

It made me wonder if there's such a thing as a 'National Throttle Day'? I can think of a few candidates for that one…unfortunately, there isn't.. I also looked to see if there was a 'National Get Away With Murder Day', which was another no, although I was offered a DVD on the subject for £11.99.

Interesting facts

Laughing for 15 minutes burns up to 40 calories.

Rats laugh when they're tickled, and the more they play together, the more they laugh. Psychologist Jack Panksepp first observed laughing rats in the 1990s; he needed special equipment to hear it, as rats' laughs are very high pitched.

Laughing Is Good for Your Relationships -Research shows that couples who use laughter and smile when discussing a touchy subject feel better in the immediacy and report higher levels of satisfaction in their relationship. They also tend to stay together longer.

On a recent shopping trip, I thought I'd treat myself to some nice new lingerie, having looked at my faded, washed with the wrong colour's underwear, hanging on the clotheshorse drying. I'd placed it strategically behind a bath towel, in case anyone looked through the lounge window. So here I am on a Saturday afternoon in the middle of a Department store perusing the 70% off sales rack. I'm hoping they've got my size left when I overheard a young man possibly early thirties at the counter beside me asking for assistance. 'I'm looking for a birthday present for my wife and I thought I'd buy her some nice underwear', he said to the sales assistant. How lovely I thought, imagining his wife's delight at receiving something nice and frilly, wrapped in tissue paper and gift-wrapped. The sales assistant was eager to assist and asked him, 'Any particular colour you think she'd like'. 'I think something delicate pink would be nice', was his reply, and 'What about her size'. It was obvious at this point he didn't have a clue and he had the assistant hold up several small sizes of frilly knickers while placing her fist inside the matching bra cups puffing them out in the hope he could gauge the approximate size of his wife. He need not have worried, his daughter probably aged about six and obviously getting bored by now, came to the rescue, and without batting an eyelid said, 'knickers for a big ar*e'. I don't know how the assistant kept a straight face, but I almost choked on my chewing gum, which landed on the floor in front of me. I apologise now if anyone was shopping in a Department store in Plymouth on 6th January and got chewing gum stuck to their shoe, but there was absolutely, no way, I was bending down to pick it up after the man and the assistant turned around to glare at me. My red face and me just kept walking.

Just remember size IS everything...

Pamper me not

I know for most people going to the hairdressers is an enjoyable experience, for me it's a nightmare. I'm not one, for sitting still for hours on end and drinking incessant amounts of coffee. Then there's the game of musical chairs, one for consultation, one for a wash, one for colour and cut & maybe another to sit in while they dry your hair. The annoying thing is, you're spent 10 minutes warming the seat up, only to be moved to another chair.

Just because I'm having my hair done doesn't mean when you offer me a magazine I want to see the latest crazy hairstyle or a master class in English Country Garden's how to prune your camellias or prop up your peas and the ultimate no, no, for me is being asked, do I want a head massage. I see women revelling in this, but in my case, I just want to wash and go, and no that's not an advert for a brand of shampoo. I often wonder who invented the idea of putting tin foil in your hair? I'm telling you now, the feel and sound of wet tinfoil being dragged through your hair is not a pleasant one.

The last time I went to the hairdressers I bumped into an ex-work colleague who was just leaving after having her hair done. We had a lovely chat, and I commented on how lovely her hair looked. She looked at me smiling then whispered that she said she was going home to wash it, as she never liked how it was done. I think it's me; I'm just not into this entire pampering thing. My sister convinced me, to go for a Spa Treatment when we were on holiday. I was reluctant, but after much deliberation agreed, as she said we could go in together and it would be fine. I'd looked at the menu of treatments and decided to go for some sort of body wrap. Walking into the place it had a feeling of tranquillity, we walked past the trickle of waterfalls and through the rose garden and a sense of calmness surrounded me. That stopped immediately when two women who looked like all in wrestlers appeared from behind a door and immediately separated us. I felt a sense of urgency that only a co-joined twin could feel. Ten minutes later, my bathrobe lay on a chair beside me.

It had been the only thing that had provided me with any form of security; now it had been replaced with a sheet that she moved about a lot exposing different parts of the body at any given time. I was lied face down, with my head through a hole in the massage bed, looking at the floor below me and thinking how the hell did I get into this. I glanced at the door a couple of times, thinking, maybe I could make a run for it, but at this point, I was partly covered in clay. What followed next, I can only describe as an encounter with copious amounts of clay and a remake of The Mummy. A trip to the local hospital minor injuries unit would have seen far less bandages used. The unwrapping later seemed to take forever, and after lying there for 60 minutes, what emerged from the bandages was I.

Did I feel any lighter? Well, my pocket certainly did, I think it was lighter by about 100 Euros. I can honestly say that I felt no different to when I use my usual brand of Lotus Flower and Cherry Blossom body butter, which smells delicious and for which 100 Euro I could probably have bought a year's supply for. My sister emerged laughing and said, 'Did you enjoy it'? My reply was 'It's off my bucket list'. Would I do it again? Probably not.

Willy's & Rainbows

Well, it's a gloomy Friday in January and it's my birthday. I was hoping for a relaxing day, and as always, it starts off well. I stayed at my son's last night, so I'm woken up by my beautiful 3-year-old Granddaughter, earlier than I would have chosen, but anyway….lovely cards, present and a trip for lunch into town with my son.

While in town I remembered I needed a leaving present for someone at work. I'd already bought a present but wanted a joke one to go with it. Walking through town, I noticed a shop that sold bizarre gifts and immediately knew I could get what I wanted in there, my son came into the shop with me. I'm looking at all the quirky stuff when a man's voice behind me says 'Can I help you, are you looking for anything in particular'. Without hesitation I replied 'a stress relief Willy', much to my son, who in his 30's embarrassment. For anyone who doesn't know what it is, it's is an object you can squeeze when you're feeling stressed, in this case, I wanted one shaped like a penis. 'Oh, I think we've sold out he said, but my colleague will be here in a minute I'll ask him'. A few minutes later his male colleague comes out from the back of the shop. 'Do we have any of those large stress relief Willy's left' he asks him. 'No', was his reply, 'they're trendy and sell out fast'. I looked at him and said 'Do you have a small one then? He started laughing and said 'yes, but it's not for sale'. 'Mother, I can't take you anywhere', my son said, as the assistant and I started laughing. His final piece of advice was to try next door. Coming out of the shop we noticed the Anne Summers shop next door, but for some reason, my son wouldn't come in with me. A couple of minutes later I came out happily swinging my bag with a Willy in it and change from a tenner, admittedly it wasn't the biggest.

The drive home later was going fine, until I'm travelling along a 40MPH Rd and a woman decides to pull out of a side Rd straight in front of me. How I stopped, I don't know. I remember hearing the screech of my tyres and swerving to avoid the car, which pulled out and turned right in front of me. It was like watching a movie in slow motion. I looked at the sign; and noticed she'd just pulled out of the Crematorium, if she's not more careful she'll be in there herself very soon. The man driving behind her, now waiting to come out of the crematorium shook his head in disbelief as she continued, without stopping. If there's such a thing as a near miss that was it! I drove the next 20 miles with legs like jelly and I could hear my heartbeat...

After the shock wore off a bit, my drive continued without incident. I listened to a little music and as I looked out of my window in between the rain showers, straight in front of me was a big bright rainbow. The best thing about it was the end of the rainbow as it appeared to be directly coming down directly in front of me on the road. I drove through it, but wasn't taking any chances looking for that pot of gold, I figured having had such a near miss and not being hurt, I'd already got my pot of gold.

The Hospital Patient

It's 11.30am, I know because I've been watching the hands on the clock turning slowly since I was woken up at some unearthly hour for my blood taken by a student vampire. My only distractions for the day so far, have been medical staff prodding, poking and nodding their heads, muttering as they left me and the rattle of the tea trolley along the hospital corridor. Flora in the bed next door has taken to doing loud under the bedcover, noises that being deaf she can't hear but everyone else can. I would have put the TV on to cover them up, but someone's left the remote control just out of reach.

I've been left a menu to fill in for tomorrow, but no pen! Am I supposed to write in blood? I must say, the menu choices sound pretty good. However, the proof is in the pudding as they say, which happens to be rhubarb crumble a favourite of mine, although banoffee pie sounds good too. I've been told I may go home today, but the thought of rhubarb crumble makes me want to stay a bit longer.

I'm getting used to the routine now; actually, if you cut out the prodding, poking and constant embarrassing near misses with a bedpan, it isn't too bad. Three meals a day, a clean, warm room and I can see rabbits through the window. I certainly don't feel lonely in here. From my bed, I listen to the everyday conversations of those around. It's like a real-life TV soap, staff being actors without their knowledge. I'm privy to the inner lives of those who pass by.

It's almost disappointing when a visitor arrives, like when you're watching a TV programme and you have a power cut or the phone rings and you just can't leave it. Here I'm sat mid eavesdropping when someone pops their head around the door, 'I bet you're glad to see me, aren't you? I manage a wry smile. What do I say? 'Actually no, just close the door on your way out', 'second thoughts leave it open a little. I'm just listening to the important bit…ahh she had a baby girl'. I'll no doubt hear more later. The only consolation of visitors is I usually end up with a collection of recycled magazines, which gives me something to do, a bunch of reduced-price flowers, you can see where they've peeled the yellow sticker off and a punnet of half-eaten grapes, or at least they are by the time they leave.

Occasionally someone might think outside the box and bring me something useful in; woe betides it be nail scissors, they'll be put in solitary confinement, pending my risk assessment. After thirty years of cutting my own fingernails, I fear I'll be declared unfit, probably be supervised with them and the offending items removed once the jobs are done, just in case....

The smell of food wafts down the corridor. I can't think for the life of me what I've ordered for lunch. I hear activity in the corridor and see the hustle and bustle as staff deliver trays of food in all directions. The conversation focuses only on food now, except for the man in bed 6, Henry, whose decided now's a good time to go to the toilet. I can't see him, but I recognise the sound of his slippers shuffling as he walks. Lunch is almost over before he returns.

The Doctor's seen me this morning. I'm waiting for my results to see if I can go home. The Occupational Therapist or Occupational Terrorist as I like to call her, came to see me yesterday. She's making sure I can manage at home. I've watched her victims passing my door daily, pausing only to catch their breath before the next onslaught of punishment, or that's what it feels like, although I know her intentions are good. I'm fit enough to go home now I can climb a flight of stairs and make a drink, although she says I won't be doing any running for a while, there's a surprise.

The cleaner's been in, my rooms looking lovely, well as far as hospital rooms can do. I've asked someone to move my flowers as they've wilted in the heat. I'm washed, dressed, eaten lunch, apparently, someone else's as they mixed the trays up. It didn't really matter because neither of us could remember what we'd ordered, although I must say I was pleased with her chocolate trifle. I'm sure my fruit compote will sort her bowels out later.

That's good…. I overhear them saying the missing cat's been found, taken in by some elderly couple after finding her injured from a fight, sounds like reimbursing the vet bills going to hurt…

My transport home's finally arrived. They're insisting pushing me in a wheelchair to the ambulance. As they escort me off the premises, I recycle 'again' my magazines giving them to a patient I pass on the way out. 'Sorry', I shout as I notice his white stick further along, propped up against a chair.

Bugger, I think as I'm pushed past the kitchen. I wonder who will be eating my rhubarb crumble tomorrow?'

Dog meat sandwiches and Life's a bed Of Roses

My van's getting a little hot at the moment with the recent hot weather, not that I'm complaining, it's just that if I'm camping alone, I don't really want to leave my windows open at night. I went online and ordered a fan/air cooler. I should have known, my great Auntie always said, 'you get what you pay for'. I was expecting a wind turbine but got a little puff of air. I now have a hot van with hot blowing air…In fact, the only good thing about the fan is they delivered it on time.

Everyone's gardens are looking lovely. I've pressure washed the patio, then the van and the house windows, in fact, anything I could while it was turned on, including an unfortunate passer-by, had it been colder outside she might have been a little less forgiving. I don't have a garden as such, just a paved area and my 2 hanging baskets outside my front door, which I bought at a reduced price of £2.50 each at Morrisons. I spotted them, grabbed them quickly and hung them on the front of my trolley, before anyone else had a chance to, then watched my trolley like a hawk in case anyone came near it.

I'm jumping in the van armed with an empty 4-pint water carrier, (posh name for milk carton), as I've been asked by a friend to water her hanging baskets while she's on holiday…this is quite a challenge for me. I'm not a gardener, which is why I never risk paying a lot for plants. I am to the gardening world, a plant pessimist, a serial killer with years of crimes behind me. I didn't have the heart to tell her this at the time of her request, but I'm feeling the pressure a bit now. I'm up against the heat and I'll be fighting for basket survival.

Why is it when you're in work you can think of a million things to do at home and when you're at home you either forget or lack the motivation to do them…. I suppose it's because most of it's the mundane stuff like clean the oven, do the ironing. Wouldn't it be great if your house was self-cleaning? Imagine that walking in from work and everything was gleaming…no mucky grill pan and no need for a bog brush.

I think a trip to Specsaver's may be required again soon. I went to make a sandwich for my lunch giving myself a break from cleaning my kitchen cupboards out and it almost consisted of cold meat and thick cut dark marmalade instead of sandwich pickle. Talking of sandwiches, I once made a dog meat sandwich for an ex. It was very late at night and he'd been out drinking. He returned a little worse for wear and almost fell through the door as I opened it, he'd forgotten his key. Actually, he hadn't he just couldn't get his hand to coordinate with his pocket. Once inside, I guided him to the bathroom. I wasn't taking any chances. He then decided he wanted a sandwich, following some incoherent, demanding ranting, about how I was the woman and I should make him a sandwich. I decided to oblige to his demands. Voila, a few minutes later one lovingly prepared, thick cut, deep filled, beef tripe, dog meat sandwich. I vaguely recall throwing a bit of cucumber in for texture and to distract from the taste. He was quite happy to see I'd conformed to his demands, as I brought in his sandwich and he muttered something about me being such a good person while shoving it in his mouth. I waited for a reaction, but he was so drunk he didn't even notice. All I can say is beware of ordering room service after midnight.

I have just had a message a minute ago… It appears my friend, although she hasn't actually said it to me, may have heard of my crimes to plants haha!. My duties to water her hanging baskets have been withdrawn, my services to horticulture are no longer required (phew)….It is a blessing indeed, for the plants…..Meanwhile, my one and only strawberry plant, which last week was looking great, has flatlined and been given last rites….

To Do Or Not To Do?

I've just had a couple of days off work and to keep myself motivated. I decided to write a '**To Do List**' and get on with stuff. I thought it would help me feel a sense of achievement as I cross things off it. Here it is...

Sort out handbags

Clean under stairs cloakroom

Clean van

Write the next week's blog...

Make a phone call to a Tax office.

Clean bathroom

I'm not sure I like the look of this '**clean**' word, it's appearing far too often.... Five minutes in and already I'm not sticking to my list in the right order, filling a bucket with hot soapy water to clean the van. Standing at only 5ft 2' tall the van towers over me and fifteen minutes later I've already done 5 buckets of water, wish I'd never started, and will never in a million years reach the bird cr*p on the roof. At least that's my exercise for the day.

Sort out handbags....

I've only a few handbags compared to some. I decided to start with the big bag I use daily. I reach in, noting that at least it's not sticky, so no unwrapped, half sucked boiled sweets lurking about, always a good start. The contents are as follows...

- A flask with a small amount of coffee from several days ago, which is now wearing a fur coat.

- One pen that doesn't work

- One pen top (that doesn't belong to the pen above)

- One lip gloss (dried up)

- 3 empty sweet wrappers

- An empty glass case

- One pair of spare knickers (I always carry a spare pair, since someone sh*t themselves at work and had to walk to their car looking like John Wayne)

- A teaspoon with traces of dried lunchtime yoghurt on it, peach I believe.

- A staff work rota

- A long piece of toilet roll. I only buy tissues if I'm having visitors, although I did once walk in work with a long piece trailing out of my bag..

- Half a pay slip..

- A diary from last year although reading through it, it certainly wasn't a year to remember..

- Lip balms three of, aloe vera, coconut & vanilla & one that smells of menthol.

- A small Phillips screwdriver

- A notebook

- Deodorant

- 87p in loose change …you'll be amazed what you can buy with it

- My purse

- A pen that works

- An empty Turkish Delight wrapper

- 4 bits of fluff & a small piece of bread which looks like something extinct, there's a sultana attached to it….

I search the house, frantically looking for my glasses, before finally finding them on my head. I carefully go through the bag and soon the sweet wrappers, yoghurt spoon, dodgy pen, screwdriver and lip-gloss have gone. The spare knickers have been replaced with ones not attached to fossilised Hot X bun crumbs & bits of fluff. The flask is as good as new. I've put a packet of diarrhoea tablets in the bag, as I keep getting flashbacks of the poor woman trying to make a sharp exit John Wayne style from the toilet to her car.

I've had enough of bags so onto my next 'To Do'…

Make a phone call to a Tax Office!

I've decided tomorrow will be a 'good day', to phone the tax office, it's not exactly phone a friend, is it?

Coffee, 2 digestive and toilet break and I'm raring to go again....

Clean under stairs cloakroom

I open the door; there's a toilet in there somewhere. I can't actually see it. I pull out a baby car seat and some fishing gear. Why do I have so much of other people's cr*p in here? An empty cardboard box, a large bag of paperwork, I've just found my lost passport phew! I move the bag to one side; there it is looking me in the eye, the big white beast. I knew there was a toilet in there somewhere. I feel like I've been on safari and released a wild animal into freedom. My toilet is 'Born Free', Oh the joy it must have felt having all that weight is taken off it and a good old clean up with bleach ahh!!!

Finally, Clean the bathroom

By this point, I feel like the two women on the TV programme 'How clean is your house', except my bathrooms not, and I've lost the urge to clean now.

Am I Menopausal?

I was watching a TV Programme and thinking I'm the right age to be Menopausal, being the wrong side of 21 and having lots of symptoms and ailments, diabetes, high cholesterol, anaemia, so how would I know if I'm Menopausal. I decide to do my own research, without the aid of medical intervention and unnecessary probing. You know the scene; you go in the doctors for an ear, nose and throat infection and before you know it your overdue smear test is glaring you in the eye on the doctor's computer screen and there's no escape. Legs akimbo, it's all over in minutes and then they give you some excuse about not prescribing anything for your throat infection. I thought a good place to start would be to read the medication inserts, you know the paper ones stuffed inside the medication packets, usually in writing so small you wished you'd gone to Specsavers Secondly, and this is the big one, I read the symptoms and side effects so that I could start a process of elimination, this was, a big mistake! After taking medication for five years, this was the first time I'd read the enclosed advice leaflet (I can hear the tuts). So, I start reading, section one, that seems ok, a straightforward 'what are the tablets used for'? I'm starting to relax with my steaming mug of coffee and sugar-free biscuits (don't believe anyone who says they taste good they don't). I'm sitting there in my recently purchased Specsavers glasses (buy one get one free) and a new symptom appears from nowhere...(palpitations)!

Have you ever had palpitations? It's not a nice feeling. Anyway, for a few seconds, my life flashed before me. I felt myself fading but knew I had to stay with it, as the Kleeneze woman was due any minute and I owed her a fiver for some toilet seat wipes that actually I didn't really want, but I felt sorry for her. My eyes continued darting rapidly across to section two 'What you need to know before you take these tablets', and the immortal words 'do not take if,' with the awful realisation at the same time, that whatever it says, it's too bloody late for me now.

Remarkably, I am however still here and fear I may have encountered each and every one of the aforementioned side effects, on several occasions. I remember some better than others, including the itches in orifices you cannot scratch while pushing your trolley around Asda, well at least not until the aisle is clear. Even then you look around and watch for the cameras, because you know, as you look around to check no one is looking, they'll see you acting suspiciously and probably pick you up for shoplifting.

They also never tell you, that most of these medications give you the shits. They let you wait to find out until you're stood at a bus stop, other people wonder why you look like you're having hot flushes and you're pulling screwed up facial expressions at them. Then the bus that you've waited for an hour and a half for arrives and you can't get on it. Instead, you wave to the people leaving on the bus before you dart behind the nearest bushes with whatever you can find to deposit your last night's salad in. I warn you now beware of cheap carrier bags.

Anyway, I come to read what is almost the final part of this truly informative, life-changing, thought-provoking, medication leaflet which says 'If', and I repeat 'If' you have any side effects seek medical advice.

I have now made appointments next week with the Doctor, Pharmacist and Nurse and I will be seeing the Midwife on Wednesday.

***Am I Menopausal?** Who knows…?*

Where there's a blame

Dear Customer Service...

I wish to complain about the packet of breakfast cereal I bought recently. It says on the box that the beneficial effect is obtained with a daily intake of 10g of wheat bran fibre, which are 2 biscuits. I feel that despite eating 2 biscuits every morning, I'm not getting the benefits you are promising. Every time I take 2 biscuits out of the packet, even with the gentlest approach, I am missing corners or worst still they break in half. Can you please advise the best way to avoid breakage and compensate me for the missing 3g of fibre?

I have tried on more than one occasion to open your easy ring pull cartons of milk, that you say are disabled friendly. Can you please inform me what type of disability you are referring to, as I do not appear to fit your criteria? I enclose photographic evidence and my dry-cleaning bill…

I was in your shop on Tuesday and bought a bumper bag of broken biscuits. Many of the biscuits were stuck together with chocolate and I was disappointed to find that two of the biscuits were not broken. Can you please supply a refund…?

I recently purchased a large tin of peaches in your store that was buy one, get one free. I do not have space in my cupboard for two large tins of peaches, so is it possible to have the tin I bought for half price? The man from Del Monte says 'Yes'. Do you?

I recently bought a set of new luxury bath towels from you and put them in my bathroom. I've noticed since, that one of them has a spider on it. How do I return it?

I was asleep in bed upstairs when one of your delivery drivers rang my doorbell. I was unable to get to the front door quick enough and the driver got back in his van. I ran outside and managed to get my parcel from him, but I'm now being charged with indecent exposure. Can you please speak to my solicitor so she can get to the bottom of this?

I have always been satisfied with your two-ply soft and loveable toilet paper. However recently I have noticed that my fingers seem to go through it. I have enclosed the offending piece in question. Please be careful when opening the enclosed envelope.

I recently bought a pot of strawberry yoghurt. While I was having lunch with a friend at my house, she pointed out that it was full of live active bacteria. Although I couldn't see any movement myself, I thought I would write and let you know.

My partner and I tried out one of the beds in your showroom and were extremely satisfied. However, since it was delivered to our house, we are not sleeping and do not seem to be receiving the same level of satisfaction.

'It appears we are a Nation of complainers; some are genuine, others are out of this world ridiculous. Be wary of signs saying 'satisfaction guaranteed'.

Exercise a bad thing or not?

I really do try hard to be healthy, of course, I'm going to slip up when on holiday and faced with a great big bowl of whipped cream, strawberries & ice cream looking at me and begging to eat me, but my greatest downfall is exercise, except for having the endurance to eat the whole ice cream sundae…it was a hell of a test, one which had to be done, but I passed it with flying colours..

I've just read a saying, 'what you eat in private you wear in public', Oops, I don't think this outfit's going to look good and yes, my bum will look big in this now.

When I say exercise, what I really mean is the total and utter, distinct lack of it. If anyone knows how to avoid exercise, it's me. I have a list of ready to hand excuses for when someone suggests anything remotely connected to it…Swimming? Better not, it's getting cold now and I don't want to get flu, I've had it once and never again. Funny, I never say, that was donkey's years ago and I have a flu jab every year. I am trying though, and earlier this year I bought a pushbike. My first attempt at riding it, I rode on the pavement, I thought it best not to go onto the road. I noticed immediately, I'd developed a wobble in my rear end, it felt like my legs didn't belong to my body. My bike and bum wobbling down the road didn't go unnoticed, especially by the man on the mobility scooter, who overtook me shortly after I stopped for a rest. I think it was quite cruel of him, to be laughing as he passed me, although at the time I was more concerned with my heartbeat, which had significantly increased, along with my blood pressure and colour changes, which were somewhere between the pink and purple spectrum. All I can say is that on this day I made someone smile, very brightly.

Then there are the elastic stretch bands that cost very little. Three large bands in different colours and different tension strengths. The biggest problem I encountered was opening the plastic packaging, which they were in. In the end, it required a pair of scissors and very careful manoeuvres. It didn't help that once open; the exercises inside were written in Japanese with no translation and the pictures looked more like something from the Karma Sutra. Thinking about it now, for a few pounds, these large elastic bands could indeed have multiple uses.

I tried horse riding, but it was such an ordeal for me getting on the horse, that the horse was traumatised before we even moved, and after half an hour in the saddle, I walked like John Wayne for three days.

Then of course whatever you're doing, you've got to look the part. There's no point turning up at the local Gym wearing high heels when you need the very latest aerodynamic, clima cool, gel, tubular runner trainers and pecs enhancing Lycra…

My friend bought me a Fitbit…not that he was saying I needed to get in shape nor was he? However, once I discovered that I could manage to walk over the daily-recommended number of steps, I became complacent. It was also a little disconcerting at work, as not being allowed to wear anything on our wrists in the hospital, I decided to wear it around my ankle. I think some people who spotted it thought I was tagged and doing community service.

Exercise is big business and costs lots of money, from Gym & leisure memberships to protein shakes, diet supplements and the vast range of equipment to vibrate your hips, stretch your body and shake your booty. However, for all of this you need 2 things, willpower, (don't think I know him) and motivation. Remember Mr Motivator, he could shake his maracas and so early in the morning too..

Anyway, as the Japanese say, 'Tameshite kesshite akiramenai', which simply means, 'Never give up trying'.

Cucumber Sandwiches or All you can eat?

It's 4.20am and I'm woken up by the sound of two drunken idiots opening my large metal gate at the front of the house, which makes an enormous racket. I'm hoping they decide to run all the way around the house, because it's dark and if they do; I know they'll run into my trailer and probably end up with a tow bar between their legs. Imagine the phone call to the ambulance service. I've got a man. He's run into my trailer. Can he hitch a ride to the hospital? Yes, I know the old ones are the best…. My heart's pounding as I go outside to close the gate.

This week I attended the leaving do of a work colleague. I took her a present, consisting of, a make up bag (conventional present) and a Willy shaped stress reliever I'd bought earlier, which thinking about it now, having left work she may not need it. They had no big ones left when I bought it, so I had to get regular one, which to me looks a bit on the small size. Anyway she's having a laugh and a good old squeeze, so I guess she likes it. Presents over and we have afternoon tea to look forward to. This is my second afternoon tea in a week, so it looks like I'll need to dust off my gym card. It's a far cry from the quintessentially English dainty cucumber sandwiches, scones with jam & cream and fruitcake. Today's afternoon teas have become a far more elaborate affair with mini desserts, glasses of Prosecco, Champagne & petit fours, I almost said petit pois. I know it's daft, but one of the things that I like most about afternoon tea, is not having to cut my own crusts off.

Prices for Afternoon Tea these days vary from acceptable to ruddy ridiculous, but as long as people are willing to fork out as they say then 'kaching'. A quick look at Harrods Afternoon Tea Menu reveals their price is presently £35 for assorted sandwiches, scones with jam & cream and a choice of dessert. The tea is served on Wedgwood china or £47 with a glass of champagne. If you want their 'exclusive' cup of tea as opposed to their 'regular' cup of tea, expect to pay an extra £6. So if partaking in a glass of bubbly and the 'best' tea it could set you back £53 per person, although, you could just have the scones with jam & cream that will set you back a mere £15. I think I'm in the wrong job. I'm getting the Wedgwood out. Anyone for afternoon tea at mine?

I've never been to Harrods, except once, when as a 13-year-old girl I went on a school trip to London. It's coming back on the coach, I remember the most. I'd bought a pair of souvenir knickers depicting London on them. Unfortunately they never made the return home with me. They were last seen being catapulted up the inside of the coach whilst travelling at 60MPH on the M6 somewhere near Birmingham.

At the other end of the scale, there's the emergence of the 'All you can eat' buffet, quantity over quality. If ever there was a time for coronary catering this is it. You see people piling their plates so high, they're dropping stuff on the floor on the way back to their tables and what for? It's all you can eat buffet so you can revisit time and time again perhaps they don't get the concept. I was thinking of new advertising slogans for the 'All you can eat buffet', although I don't think it would attract many customers. My slogans would be…

'Eat lots, Live less'

'More for Mortality'

'Diets Die Here'

'Fatality Feasting'

So what's it to be 'Afternoon Tea' or 'All you can eat buffet'? Answers on a postcard to Mrs Blobby….

Auntie Sarah's birthday party

There it is behind your front door your invite to Auntie Sarah's birthday party. Your first thought is, how the hell am I going to get out of this, then the excuses start pouring into your head, the usual, the dog ate my invite, you have an appointment with the dentist, your stomach's upset. You know that no one will believe you. There is nowhere to hide. The venue is a few steps from your door, so apart from death, there would be no excuse that you could get away with for not attending. Even with death, you'd have to be cold in the ground because if you were just 'on your way out', the family would probably prop you up at a table against the bar, just so they could say how lovely it was that so many people attended. The buffet will as usual consist of crisps (plain), a few sausage rolls; curled sandwiches and Gateaux specially defrosted for the occasion.

Ok, I think, 'be positive, perhaps this party will be different'. My boyfriend at the time reluctantly agreed to come. I don't think he really knew what he was letting himself in for, or particularly wanted to, but I didn't want to go alone and I thought it would be good to share the boredom with him. We hadn't been going out that long and I'd been trying really hard not to scare him off. He'd met some of the family, but so far not any of the ones that I would say are a little odd.

I couldn't decide what to buy Auntie Sarah for a present. I wanted something she'd never forget. My mind started working overtime for a minute. My thoughts went to those of an erotic nature, batteries not included, but I wasn't sure with her being a practising catholic, never married and a virgin at 63 that this was appropriate. I also had to consider that there was a strong possibility of her opening her present in front of the vicar, who I believed was attending the party. In the end, I settled for a scarf and chocolates.

The night of the party I decided to wear a pretty pink floaty dress with heels, and dangly earrings. I glanced in the mirror on my way into the party venue and I was feeling pretty impressed with what I saw, but then realised I was looking at someone else behind me.

The venue was large and echoed as people started to arrive. The DJ, a man I'd say probably retired about twenty years ago, was playing music I failed to recognise, but for the two people on the dance floor it was proving popular. I couldn't really see who they were as the glitter ball was making patterns across their faces and their erratic dance moves made it impossible to see.

The obligatory cheek kissing and greeting was going on around the room, as family members arrived having not spoken since Uncle David's wake, which at this moment in time felt like it had been the livelier of the two events. I found a table in the corner for us, hoping to go unnoticed. It was a bit like being an Orangutang with your bum on display because it wasn't long before curiosity got the better of the odd ones. Shortly after that a comment about how much weight I'd put on and was I up the duff? sent my mum into almost the quickest foxtrot I'd ever seen my dad do, in fact I'm not sure his feet touched the floor.

Auntie Sarah looked lovely, and I'm pretty sure I saw the Vicar pat her bum and wink at her, perhaps I should have gone with the other present. She looked disappointed as she thanked me for her scarf and chocolates. I almost told her what I was going to buy her, but before I had chance to say anything she was up on stage and it was time for the thank you speeches. Auntie Sarah was quietly spoken but I just about heard her say, 'Andrew and I would like to thank you all for coming', I was thinking to myself, who is Andrew? next thing the vicar slips his arm around her waist, bloody hell you kept that one quiet. After that the party seemed to liven up, everyone smiling, dancing and chatting as the camcorder scanned the room. I think the promise of a free bar for the rest of the night helped.

Four months later and Auntie Sarah and Vicar David have apparently adopted an African child and are living in a commune somewhere.

For the rest of us, it's the traditional after party viewing of the recorded nights events. Everyone gathers in the lounge and sits quietly as the tape rolls, even Granddad George is here, having been given day release from hospital. Auntie Rita and Auntie June are here.

Nieces, nephews, even the next-door neighbour and her dog. Mint humbugs are rife and apart from the odd crunching noise, you can hear a pin drop as everyone sits watching. The volume gets turned up louder because Auntie June announces she's forgotten her hearing aid. 'Oh there's me', I declare, as the video scans to me and my boyfriend talking in the corner of the room and like flies on a wall the whole room hears the words as they come out of my mouth, 'that's my Auntie Rita she's an alcoholic'….

Digital Diva

This week I've become a Digital Diva and ordered myself a new 49-inch Curved Smart TV having had enough of my old TV. It's impossible for me to understand with 2 boxes, 3 remotes and a spaghetti junction of wires, plus a trailing lead that I've caught my foot in twice. I've not a bloody clue what any of the wires are for; even trying to put the TV on is a joke. I'm waiting for a special delivery, my all singing, all dancing TV; this is going to be 'plug and go', hopefully, although anything can happen. I've waved bye-bye to my old TV and I am waiting patiently for the new one's arrival. It's a bit like being pregnant I know it's going to arrive but I'm not sure what it'll be.

In work it's been so hot; I thought I would actually melt. I arrived one morning at 6.20am to discover that a new member of staff had accidentally turned the air conditioning unit off overnight in the hospital kitchen.

It's not their fault, as they didn't know, however irate night staff was gunning for the first person that arrived in the kitchen that morning, unfortunately it was me. I could understand their frustration, as on what was probably one of the hottest nights so far the kitchen was like a sauna....one hormonal woman and a red hot kitchen do not go very well together, however the flick of a switch and normality returned, well as much as it could do. What I find really strange is that the patients are still choosing to have hot soup and hot suppers in the evening when the temperature is so hot outside....

Every so often, I like to think about the things I've done and what I'd like to do, inspiration often comes from reading about other people's lives, in particular those travelling around in their Camper vans or Motorhomes. The time is not right at the moment for me but it will come...

Social networking websites provide a little insight into people's lives. However, sometimes I think, what is my life coming to, when I read something and then sit here and consider whether or not I should answer the question. What side should you butter your potato cake on? Worse still, 200 people comment. Come on get a grip, who gives a hoot what side you butter it, if you butter it, or if you don't butter it....

Today my TV arrived. The deliveryman asked me if I was just moving in, which was quite amusing as I've been here for 15 months now. I think it's the minimalist look, it sort of confuses people. Having created enough cardboard recycling to keep a team in work, I'm feeling quite proud of myself for having set the TV all up and it's ready to go. It was pretty easy following the on screen instructions.. I don't think I've got the hang of Netflix though, as I thought I was watching a film, it turned out to be a series and I'm on episode 8 (each one was 40 minutes long) so here I am again sitting with my glass of non alcoholic wine and a bowl of strawberries waiting for the action to commence. I'm still no nearer to the truth of who did it and here's me thinking it'll be all done and dusted in a couple of hours....

Hotels 'At Your Service'

Hotels can be so different; they can make or break your holiday. Have your ever stayed in a place, where you think you've actually bought shares in it when you look at what they've charged you for a small bottle of water? Yes, me too, and one where I didn't bother with the meals, once I'd seen the chefs fingernails and monitored his incessant scratching. Fantastic family holiday! She said to me on the phone…last minute bargain; the words were ringing in my ears as we pulled up outside, what looked like a prison cellblock. We were just saying how dreadful it would be for anyone who was staying there, as they called our names out to get off the coach. Our first impression of Greek hotels was not good….

There's always something exciting about going on holiday. It's a chance to watch people. I remember, seeing a couple in Portugal. I'm assuming it was his wife, who sat on a wall having her picture taken, under a beautiful tree in the glorious Algarve sunshine. She stood up after the usual, 'say cheese for the camera', to discover it was a fig tree and her white trousers were, let's just say, incontinence springs to mind. Her husband didn't help the situation with his hysterical laughter. He was last seen being clocked around the head by his wife's handbag.

When you work in a hotel, it's totally different, discretion is required and you're never really sure, what you'll find when you open the bedroom door….

It starts with that tentative knock, then you knock a little louder, whilst muttering 'Housekeeper', then you unlock and open the door. Occasionally, the door swings open, on the startled guest who, forgot to put their hearing aid back in, or the one who was in the shower but now stands naked before you, or worse still the couple who appear to be playing twister, remember the game, on top of the bed.

Sometimes guests have gone down to breakfast, it's all you can eat buffet, so it's a chance to replenish the room toiletries and make the bed whilst they're out. I'm still a little confused, why anyone would hide 2 full bottles of washing up liquid under their duvet. Whatever the reason behind it, it was the popular green brand and I left it exactly where I found it. I read a student thread later that suggested using washing up liquid as lubrication. All I can say is please don't try this at home, unless you don't mind a foam party. I fear it won't turn out well. Other suggestions on the thread, included ketchup, which may explain the squirted tomato sauce I found inside a drawer, honey, and finally super glue, obviously that guy wanted to stick to his girlfriend, and with about 10 seconds before it goes hard, I'm not sure any pleasure whatsoever could be gained. It would be quite entertaining for the staff at the Minor Injuries Dept at the local hospital.

Some Housekeepers are exposed to the insides of their guests' underwear, left strewn across the bedroom floor. This is not a pretty sight, touch at your own risk or better still, let the lazy devils pick them up themselves.

10.30am one morning, I'm making drinks and cutting cake for the staff break, when suddenly one of the staff, a young Turkish Guy, who spoke very little English ran into the office, shouting at me. 'Come, come, I think someone had 16-inch pizza last night' I arrived at the room expecting to find a box with a half-eaten pizza and crumbs everywhere. Instead I find a toilet blocked in a way I've never seen before and would prefer never to see again. This toilet was blocked to capacity. I knew this called for my emergency toilet resuscitator kit, which included a wooden chopping stick, 2 black bin liners to protect your arms and a bowl for the extracted matter. This was not a job for the fainthearted, and as I tried to explain what to do, my Turkish friend suddenly developed an even lesser understanding of the English Language and was last seen heading for the sign that said public bar this way. I didn't really fancy the chocolate cake after that…

The saying 'You get what you pay for springs to mind'. A couple was complaining to the receptionist that their hotel room was not up to standard. I wondered, was it the threadbare carpet around the toilet, or the ceiling above the bed that hardly screamed passion with missing plaster and limp wallpaper. How do you tell someone that this is one of the better rooms and to watch the bucket in the middle of the corridor on the way back as its just started raining. The lovely water feature in room 31 (water running down the inside of the shower screen from a leaky showerhead) was never truly appreciated.

The Super king duvet cover was the bane of the Housekeeper's life. Putting one on when you're only 1.524 metres tall is like trying to erect a large tent single-handedly. You can't get in the corners, without almost getting inside the duvet cover; your Fitbit thinks you've completed a marathon. Then after the marathon you realise the guests are only there for one night and you're in the marathon again tomorrow. Worse still you're half way in and someone knocks on the door and you look like a ghost at Halloween.

My top tips for having a great holiday…

Always check the chef's fingernails

If it sounds too good to be true, it usually is

Always look before you sit down

If the housekeeper knocks on the door answer it, or she's coming in

If you're going to give a tip, make it worthwhile, three pence and half a chewing gum, does not really count

If you're an Housekeeper

Always wear gloves

Be prepared for surprises or shocks

The customer is always right (not)

Some people are tight bast*rds!

Remember tomorrows' washing is best left unseen…

Our John's Shed

Lurking at the foot of the garden the challenge awaits. I've been training for days for this, and now at last the moment is here. Fifteen squats and three minutes jogging on the spot and I've warmed up for the long awaited event. A gauntlet previously thrown down by my son, a challenge so daunting, that he could not face it alone. So on a mild November morning at 9am after much anticipation, let the battle commence. ' I am ready'; I declare as the door swings open on the shed. I'm ready to face the task of de cluttering. My son knows that I'm brutal, this is a de clutter to the death and it won't be mine.

Bin bags and rubber gloves to hand, I enter the shed. I am past the point of no return. I know this is not the time to let my arachnophobia stand in the way of progress. I glance sideways, and notice a spider's web is missing its maker and I suspect that sometime soon we may meet eye to eye, or worst still, the spider will suddenly decide to wander uninvited across my arm, leg or any uncovered body part. It is for that reason alone, that my choice of clothing, a white paper all in one body suit provides reassurance that I am almost, entirely spider proof.

My mummified body bears resemblance to a forensic investigator and as I turn to face the challenge, I see the neighbour standing watching from his bedroom window. I want to draw a chalk body outline on the grass just to watch his face and give the local church something to gossip about over morning coffee.

I step deeper into the unknown, treading carefully and moving boxes with such trepidation you'd think they contained crystal chandeliers. I notice movement. I pause momentarily, before realising that a leaf has just blown in. I release a small gasp of breath, relieved that it's nothing more.

I've told my son that his request for my help may cause alarm, and did wonder whether I should get him to sign a disclaimer before I start. I begin to brutally experience and eradicate his life through boxes upon boxes.

I begin my quest with four piles, one pile to keep (this will not happen often), one to take to the charity shop, one to recycle and finally, one pile to throw away, ditch, dump, tip or whatever you like to call it. I begin the process by tossing to one side a rather foul looking ornament. It is retrieved quickly and I'm informed it's being kept for sentimental reasons. Personally I'd have been traumatised to have received it in the first place and start to wonder about my son's mental state.

The shed is full of boxes and as I open each one, it tells a story, some happy, some sad. I find myself travelling through time, on a mission to save the good and eradicate the bad, the less interesting, or those that have just gone mouldy because they were left outside. I see their engagement photos, and the Hen Party photos. I notice as I look down at the picture, a man's bare bottom. I'm not quite sure what he's wearing, and I looked at it from several angles, but there are feathers involved.

The wedding pictures and other events like graduation and birth of a baby girl, all grace the 'keep' pile. Other boxes were not so lucky, although I did keep three boxes of cat ashes, found in the corner under the vacuum cleaner and Christmas balls. 'RIP', Pebbles, Smudge and Sooty.

Fridge magnets had compulsory removal orders served on them and were dumped, except one, which I saw my son hide quickly in his pocket. Anything broken or parts missing was also destined for the dump.

I remember once going to a jumble sale, where they had a toy stall, on the stall was a doll with no head, now call me old fashioned, but even for 50p this doll was not going to sell. So I asked the stallholder just out of curiosity and to see if she was aware of what she was selling. 'How much for the doll with no head'? She looked up at me, and without batting an eyelid said, '50p but if you'd prefer one without legs you can have one for 20p'. I left with an empty bag, but a smile on my face.

Today I ventured into the home of a significant number of black bodied, crawling, sometimes running and occasionally scary spiders, and numerous woodlice but I survived. I'm covered in dirt and hypothermia is about to set in but my mission here is complete, and as the door closes for the last time, I see a spider run under it.

Amazing fact - The silk in a spider's web is five times stronger than a strand of steel that is the same thickness. A web made of strands of spider silk is as thick as a pencil and could stop a Boeing 747 jumbo jet in flight. Scientists still cannot replicate the strength and elasticity of a spider's silk.

It's a mystery

Every so often, sometimes it happens quite frequently. I get the urge to run away. It's like someone puts this thought in my head, and it won't go away. Perhaps that's why over the years I've felt the need to keep moving house, sometimes only half a mile up the road. Anyway friends have stopped sending me New Home Cards (I suppose 23 is a bit excessive). My Auntie asked me last year specifically, for a new address book for Christmas, just before I moved again in March. If anyone is thinking of moving, de cluttering as you go, is the key to success. I know, having packed my entire last house up in less than 2 hours.

I remember going into the house of an old man in 2013 and seeing a line of boxes going all the way up the hall. He'd recently moved into the property and I said 'I see you haven't finished unpacking then' and offered to help him. He told me that those boxes were packed in

1952 and had been on three house moves since and had never been unpacked. He couldn't remember what was in there. I felt like I was suddenly possessed with obsessive-compulsive disorder. I so badly wanted to get into those boxes instead I had to settle for tea and a bun he'd made himself. I did say that the chances of him needing whatever was in there were remote and perhaps he should get rid of them. He smiled at me; I knew they were going nowhere.

I don't know where this desire to move even comes from, but it's like a dog with a bone when it starts. It's not a desire to go to any particular place, or to escape anything; it's just an urge to run. I know I can't run. I hated running in my school days, many years ago, I was always last at cross-country, except on the odd occasion someone wasn't well and they were struggling, then I stood a chance and sometimes on a good day I came next to last. Running was then followed by the embarrassment of after sports communal showering, something I loathed.

Perhaps if anyone is looking for a Getaway driver this could be my new calling, at least then there'd be a purpose and somewhere to go as long, as I didn't get arrested. I don't think I could survive in prison, although some of the documentaries make it look more appealing than some hotels you see these days.

I like the idea of Bonny & Clyde though, except the bit where they killed people, or the bit where they got ambushed and shot to death…I suppose I just like the idea of lovers on the run. Bonnie wrote poetry and 2 weeks before her death she wrote a poem for her mother that spoke of her and Clyde's death…for that reason alone any poetry I write, will not include things about my death until I am ready to meet my maker… Oops just realised I did write something a couple of weeks ago, perhaps I should say goodbye now.

My mum always said I should have been a gypsy because of all my house moves. I did purchase a caravan earlier this year, with the intention of doing it up, and sometime in the future travelling far and wide. Perhaps it was the driving rain and high winds on the day I collected it or the bits that kept dropping off on the way back, or the fact that there was no way I would ever be able to reverse it, if I had to. It was a quick purchase and an even quicker sale, of which I have no regrets. I still however have Trixie my beloved camper van in which I spent five nights in Oldham last February, to say I was a little unprepared for the cold weather was an under statement. On the first night I snuggled down in my PJ's at about 10pm drinking hot chocolate and browsing the internet thinking this is so lovely, by midnight I think I was wearing all the clothes I could find and looked like an Eskimo, red nose included. I'd forgotten how cold it gets up North.

Can you imagine if the camper van could talk 'it'd probably say 'oh no, where are we going now?. 'I do wish she wouldn't do that in here'. 'Why doesn't she wash me', 'who drew that p*nis on me', and 'arrgghhh watch out' ha ha!

If anyone is moving house and needs help de cluttering or packing I know the ideal person, but be prepared I'm brutal.

Tenerife Here We Come!

I'm getting ready for my holiday. Seven nights in Tenerife starting this Friday. I'm going with my sister Julie. I've been exercising in preparation, as I'll need to be fit, not because of all the walking we'll be doing, more because of her high expectations of me. I know I'll be loaded like a packhorse with her suitcases and probably have to turn down her covers in the evening. Actually we'll have great fun and I'll keep you all updated…

It's her birthday today, 'Happy Birthday'. You can stop pretending now, that it's your birthday every time you go out. I refer to the photo evidence in London earlier this month, when she told everyone it was her birthday and got a free dessert, she didn't say that it had been three weeks earlier.

I remember years ago, going out for a meal with a boyfriend and his mother on my 20th birthday. We were sitting having dinner quietly in the Italian Restaurant when the kitchen doors suddenly swung open. Two men playing guitars came out singing '21 today', followed by someone carrying a lit birthday cake. I could have died of embarrassment as the whole restaurant began singing. I did feel it would have been rude not to eat the cake and I did tell his mother off later.

Why do we put candles on a birthday cake?

Putting candles on birthday cakes is a long time tradition. Ancient Greeks often burned candles as offerings to their gods and goddesses. Putting candles on a round cake to symbolize the moon was a special way to pay tribute to Artemis, the Greek moon goddess. Candles signify moonlight.

Corny joke - A man walks into a bakery. All the cakes in the shop are a pound except for one, which costs two pounds. So he asks the baker "Why is it two pounds? the baker replies. "That's Madeira cake."

Anyway, I've started packing my suitcase for Tenerife and I'm praying this time it won't chewed up by the airport conveyor belt. I am still traumatised from last year when my suitcase was chewed to bits. I couldn't believe how badly it was damaged. I took photographs when I returned home to my sister's house, so I could claim compensation for the case and other ruined items. Unfortunately for me, my sister also decided to take some photographs of my suitcase, which she posted on Facebook, but not before adding something phallic looking to the contents which she left hanging out of my suitcase. I have yet to get revenge.

I usually do a list of all the holiday essentials so I don't forget anything and I'm always ready the week before, non-of this throw your stuff in your suitcase at the last minute. Looking at some of the most bizarre things that people pack in their suitcases I read that one man always packs a fire extinguisher, so much for his weight allowance; he can't leave much for clothes, a naked fireman maybe? Other bizarre things people pack include, pet ashes, a deceased pet that had been stuffed and someone from Devon couldn't sleep without the noise of a ticking clock so always carried a clock onboard with her. The ticking noise may alarm some passengers, for me it's usually a calculator, slippers (for on the beach) as I don't like the wind on my toes and teabags for my early morning cuppa.

The last 8 days have been quite traumatic as Trixie the Campervan remains in the garage; apparently the mechanic is looking for parts. I wanted to scream at him, try harder as he stood there telling me. How long does it take? I could have taken the easy route this week and opted to get taxis to and from work but decided I probably need every penny for the garage bill, so I've become green, yes me! I've been cycling to work. This was going remarkably well, considering my last experience, when the man on the mobility scooter overtook me.

In my bid to raise some cash for the 'Trixie Garage Repair Fund' I sold some bits I had lying around the house including a steel safe. The buyer asked if I could deliver it, thinking my daughter would be able to drop it off I said yes, unfortunately for me, she couldn't so I had to strap the heavy monster to the back of the pushbike and walk into town with it. To passing motorists this must have looked pretty strange, a middle-aged woman walking up the main road with a safe hanging off the back of a pushbike, although no one stopped me. The relief I felt as I safely delivered it was immense. I thought at that point, I deserved a little treat so stopped and bought a large slice of Malteser cake, which I cycled back with.

Three Camels, a Volcano, and Slippers

This was written at 37000 feet in a plane on the way back from Tenerife over the beautiful Mount Teide. I can now confirm, without a shadow of doubt, that my sister is indeed the main culprit of any shenanigans home or away, and that I am the innocent bystander that witnesses such.

Once a year my sister and I like to do the 'sister's on tour holiday' this year we picked Tenerife. The hotel was beautiful, staff and service excellent. What could possibly go wrong?

Day 1: A stroll to the beach and into the Tourist Information Office. Big mistake…my sister asks the lady in the Tourist Information office 'Do you have any 'Golden' sandy beaches around here'? The woman shouts, 'You think our beaches are dirty, then you go to

Feurteventura', ushering us out of the door. I could probably have explained that she meant because of the volcanic sand, but I was too busy laughing. Next thing a policeman arrives on his bike, fortunately it wasn't for us...

Day 2: It's mid afternoon and we are given some deckchair tickets by a man and his girlfriend, so lie down and begin to relax in the sunshine. An hour later appears the deckchair warrior and she wants some money, pointing out the fact the tickets are non-transferable. My sister decided to leave, but at a snail's pace, and not until after she's made a phone call sitting on the deck chair much to the annoyance of the ticket warrior

Day 3: My sister went into the hotel bathroom and used the toilet, creating quite a stink; unfortunately this is just as the housekeeper arrives to clean the room. Still in the bathroom my sister emerges minutes later and says, 'it smells like sewage in there'. Without batting an eyelid, the housekeeper turns to her and says. 'It's because you're underneath the kitchen'. I'm not sure what that meant, but it made me laugh.

Did you hear about the constipated accountant? He couldn't budget.

What did Mr. Spock find in the toilet? The Captain's log.

Day 4: Having been accosted by some Jet Ski ticket tout we are being frog-marched across the harbour, before we knew it, we were wearing life jackets and we're in a speed boat being taken out into the middle of the sea. I'm the first to set off on my Jet Ski. My acceleration however was a little keen causing me to take off too fast and knock the attendant back into his boat, he cut his leg. Julie got in trouble for speeding when she got back.

The Most Common Causes of Jet Ski Accidents:

Inexperienced drivers

Operator error

Driver distractions

Reckless driving or speeding (Yes, Julie)

Lack of proper protective equipment

Lack of jet ski operator instruction and training

The Most Common Jet Ski Injuries Include:

Broken bones

Amputations

Concussions

Wrongful death

Burns

Serious neck and back injuries

Fractured ankles

Dislocated orbital sockets

Damaged ear drums

Broken wrist

Brain injuries

Spinal cord injuries

- Maybe I'll give the jet skis a miss next time!

Day 5: Walking past a shop in Los Cristianos a man shouts to my sister 'Do you want to be my Spanish wife?'. 'I have a girlfriend', she says laughing and pointing at me. At this point an entire café is looking at us, so I just reply 'Do you honestly think I could fancy that'. I was then offered 3 camels in exchange for her. I can't say I wasn't tempted. I was held back by the thought of how much each camel weighed. I decided I could probably get one camel on her extra legroom seat on the plane going home, with a bit of manoeuvring. The other 2 camels may pose a problem. I wondered if he'd let me take the one camel and barter for something else a bit more airline friendly.... It was also the thought that the camel would have to sit next to me and I may get spat on, or worse still it would want a pee. Camels pee backwards apparently, and unable to get into the WC cubicle in time or at all, it would empty its bladder in the aisle. I've heard camel pee is like syrup and I had visions of the airhostess's trolley sliding down the centre aisle at the speed of light and no duty-free sales being declared that morning. So for those reasons I declined...

Day 6: We have spent a long time at the beach and shopping and we await the 2pm courtesy bus back to the hotel. It didn't turn up; neither did the one at 3pm, so at 3.30pm we get a taxi back and head to reception to voice our complaint...the receptionist explains that actually the service back is at 1pm and 4pm.

True story - A mother-of-two fed up of waiting for late buses invoiced the company £103 for her wasted time and was given £70 back in free day passes. Elizabeth Thomas, 44, said she wasted 11.24 hours waiting for the delayed service to and from her office job in Clifton, Bristol, and was less able to spend time with her children.

Day 7: I am a little worried because of my lobster back (I got burned on day 1) my skin is now peeling and my sister's obsession with peeling skin means I may come under attack during the night.

Day 8: *I realise I've forgotten my slippers…*

It's just annoying

I'm quite a tolerant person, but there are some things that really irritate me, for example. This morning, all I wanted was one pair of black socks, sounds easy doesn't it. I open my drawer, and reach inside. I'm faced with this mound of socks, mainly black, a few girly ones, two spotty ones and a Christmas pair. So I grab two of the black socks and put them on, they are not the same colour, so I try another pair on, still not the same colour, and then another. It was like fifty shades of black, spread out on my bed. In the end I admitted defeat and wore two odd black socks....

Then there's queuing. Have you ever queued at a bus stop, waited patiently for the bus to arrive, and when it does, everyone dives past you and jumps on the bus whilst you're still picking your shopping up or folding your pram. Queuing in a shop is another one. You've been waiting ten minutes to be served, when some old dear walks past you and goes to the front of the queue. You can hear the person behind saying, 'aww bless her, she must be confused'. Is it just I? That thinks confused my ar*e, she knew what she was doing. I suppose if it was in a pub with people queuing at a bar, there might be a few fights breaking out, with rants of, 'I was here first'.

I recently bought a gift from a well known Department Store online. The gift, which I really wanted, arrived damaged, so I think ok, I'll return it. I pick up the return label and read the small print, which says I can return it in store; this is not an option as I live 35 miles away from the nearest store. The second option is to return it by post. I read the next bit twice, which says I must pay for the return myself. I feel disgruntled to say the least, this item was reduced online from £15 to £4.50 and now it's probably going to cost about £3 to send it back. I decided not to bother. I just wonder how many other faulty or damaged goods are being sold that fail to be returned because of this....

Another gripe is the way that as consumers we are being ripped off, by shrinking food, packets of crisps, tins, and bars of chocolate are all victims to this. I remember as a child, if you bought a particular chocolate bar it was huge, now either my mouth has got very large or the chocolate has shrunk dramatically. I don't think even my mouth could grow that big. What I find really funny about packets of crisps though, is the fact that they didn't reduce the size of the packet, just the amount of crisps they put in there, so now it's hunt the crisps, which are usually found clinging to the inside corner of the packet.

My final gripe of the day is, when you're walking along with not a care in the world and before you see it, it's too late; you've stepped right in it. Yes, it's the dreaded dog poo on shoe scenario. I've still to catch the person who let their Great Dane walk up to the top of my drive and do one. I didn't actually see the dog but going by the size of the present it left behind, it must have been a big dog. If this is you, beware, because I'm watching and I'll follow you home where I'll return it probably through your letterbox..

Dog poo it appears is not my final gripe, because tonight after a long day at work I came home, washed my uniform, took it out of the washing machine, put it in the tumble dryer only to discover that I had forgotten to take the tissue out of my pocket and there are white bits all over my navy blue trousers...

Holly Willoughby has interviewed a huge variety of guests during her time on This Morning, breakfast TV programme but on the 10 January 2017 her guest was a 14-and-a-half-stone Great Dane, the World's Largest Dog Freddy, all seven foot of him and fourteen and a half stone.

Holly got straight to the question we all wanted answering - How do you pick up after a dog that big?! Reply - it's a two-handed job!"

'Let's go Dogging'

'Dogging' is something I know absolutely nothing about, despite any rumours to the contrary. I'm mentioning no names but the person who suggested I write about the subject, is a past work colleague, lives in Padstow, obviously a den of iniquity and she only ever drank diet coke. The incident involving the exploding coke can and the freezer, livened-up what was, originally, a quiet day and we all learned something from the accident, mostly that we would've liked to have seen it again.

WARNING *'If you are of a sensitive nature, or are easily offended, please stop reading now'*

We should now be left with a sophisticated gathering of like-minds. Filthy, drooling but similar in our curiosity or need for gratuitous literary thrills. Where do I begin? I apologise, in advance, if I offend anyone partaking in the activity of dogging. This is not a judgement, merely, an outsider's perception of the unknown. I find my keyboard is refusing to let me type certain words and phrases. Could it be something to do with my upbringing, (angels require being brought up, too) or is it possible that my dad may read this. The good old' days gave us the flasher in the rain mac and George Formby, peeping through windows, whilst cleaning them. It seems we've evolved and there is now openness about sex. A little too open, sometimes.

Just so I know that we all understand.. The Oxford dictionary definition of the word Dogging means: -The practice of watching or engaging in exhibitionist sexual activity in a public place. The Collins Dictionary definition of Dogging is: -The practice of carrying out or watching sexual activities in semi secluded locations such as parks or car parks, often arranged by e-mail or text messages. If you're sure you wish to continue reading, it must be stated that I accept no responsibility, for injury or death, as a result of distraction, from my words.

Still want to continue? Are you sure?....

So this is my slant on what I think Dogging may be like…. I'd like you to close your eyes, if you prefer you can be blindfolded, ask your partner to do this. Make sure they can read though, otherwise the story stops here. You can remove some or all of your clothing if you like, just remember where you are though, it's not a good idea if you're queuing up in the local takeaway. If you wish to tie yourself up fluffy handcuffs are not for beginners, use whatever creates the illusion, and if using a washing line take it down first. Are you ready for this?

Imagine you are walking into a supermarket. This is a supermarket like you've never seen before; it's outside in the woods, we'll assume it's dark. You see people, walking into the supermarket with their head torches on, or if it's their first time a dimly lit hand held torch and balaclava. Wellies are not a good look. You pick up your shopping basket, have a quick look at what's on your list, and look tentatively around the aisles (for recognition purposes these are also known as trees or deep undergrowth). You browse the goods, weigh up the packaging then start shopping. You stop quickly in the medication aisle to pick up your protection, of which there are several choices, fruity, hot, textured, pleasure me, comfort and that's before you choose the size or colour. Try and avoid the glow in the dark ones unless you don't mind hundreds of spectators attracted by the large bright green pulsing light just off the A30. Then it's off to look in the fruit and veg aisle. You fumble a courgette, manhandle a few bananas, almost pop a cherry and before you know it the cucumber has had you. The baskets on the floor and you've done the splits. You look up, there are people watching, someone's called a Team Meeting and the store Manager's joining in for a quick stock take. It's the only supermarket you've ever been in where you get pissed wet through whilst shopping. The use of recycled 5p carrier bags is not recommended. The photo booth seat may need a wipe first and the security guard will happily, frisk anyone. You leave feeling very happy; you managed a big shop in one go, and got the bulkiest item passed to you on the rear seat.

'If you go down in the woods tonight you better go in disguise. If you go down in the woods tonight you're in for a BIG surprise'. That was indeed the case for Mr & Mrs Bateman, a couple in their late 80's from Scunthorpe who were on their way home from an over 60's whist drive, when their car broke down near a lay-by. No mobile phone, Mr Bateman flashed his lights at the car in front, before he knew it, the poor chap was straddled over his 1960's Morris Minor bonnet, his hand clutching tightly onto his red leather buffed interior. His wife Doris was later found handcuffed to a tree wearing her Marks & Spencer's knickers back to front, her 44DD cup bra hanging off a branch, where two magpies have since taken refuge. Interviewing the couple at their home later, they said they couldn't thank the breakdown man enough for the excellent service. Four weeks later, it appears that they have phoned in and reported a further two breakdowns since.

My research which was, not of a practical nature, opened my eyes to something that apparently goes on all around us, with this in mind, make sure your car is serviced before the dark nights start coming in case you breakdown in a lay-by, have to put your hazard lights on, think the breakdown man is here, and before you know it some half naked person has jumped on the back seat and is already panting.

If after reading this you are now interested in dogging, you'll be surprised how close to your local dogging spots are to you already. Following my research and provided my computer's not been seized and I've not been arrested I'll be back soon...

PS – Off to walk the dog (the real one)

PPS -If I do get arrested, the bail money's in a coffee jar in the kitchen.

A Tale of Biscuit Dunking

Amongst all the tedium, a beautiful thing occurred to me today. It was the discovery of how long it takes a dunked biscuit to break up and then drop into the cup of the dunker as the hot liquid penetrates, softens and crumbles the biscuit. I watched as it plopped straight into the steaming hot coffee. It became a sort of ritual or little experiment to see how long the different biscuit barrel varieties fared. Timing was crucial, chocolate fingers did pretty well, and great as stirrers too, pink wafers were not pleasant. If my life wouldn't be considered so boring, I gain great satisfaction from such a trivial task. It has become a regular tea break occurrence, behind closed doors. Competition is rife at the 10am tea break, for those with the longest lasting biscuit. Wagers are made following strict guidelines. This is indeed serious business of the biscuit variety.

Recommended breakage and dunking...

Hob Nob, 15 seconds, 5 seconds

Malted Milk, 20 seconds, 6 seconds

Ginger Nut, 32 second, 3 seconds

Fig Roll, 38 seconds, 4 seconds

Chocolate Digestive, 41 seconds, 4 seconds

Digestive, 48 seconds, 5 seconds

Chocolate Hob No, 51 second, 9 seconds

Rich Tea, 58 seconds, 4 seconds

Custard Cream, 1 minute 6 seconds, 8 seconds

Jammie Dodger, 1 minute 8 seconds, 8 seconds

Shortbread, 1 minute 20 seconds, 11 seconds

Bourbon, 2 minutes 39 seconds, 7 seconds

Oops, that's Mr Timms Chief Executive, all suited and booted, smelling like an after shave counter from some Airport Duty-Free shop. I wonder what he's doing, still trying to retrieve the soggy remains of a rich tea biscuit from the bottom of Pug with a teaspoon. Okay, it's a mug with a dog on so I call it Pug. I don't think he's seen me. The last time he was here, there was talk. Okay, break over, wash Pug, headset on and here we go.

This job is not the greatest. You ring people up every day, listening to the phone slamming down or extremities of vocabulary being bellowed down the phone at you. But it's a job, and the people who work here are lovely. The exception is, of course, Col real name Morris. It's the severe acne and the hair, a sort of basin cut, not one you'd pay for unless you were doing it for charity, intoxicated or under duress, reminds me of a colander. Miserable Morris aka Col, the only non-biscuit on the team, not even tempted by a Jammie Dodger. The only time Col smiled was when Fiona inadvertently flashed her inner thigh at him as she walks past his strategically placed fan and it caught her skirt, lifting it slightly, much to Col's approval.

'Ping' email memo arrives.... Mr Timms calls a meeting in the canteen at 10am. Bugger, all dunking on hold, something big must be happening. 'Complaint Madam sorry I can't hear you the lines a little crackly'. I saw Vinny screwed up paper in his hand and then cut the complainant off in her stride.

In between phone calls, Chinese whispers circulate, as a rather elegant dressed blond piece draped in designer clothes, Rolex watch, the longest ever finger nails painted bright red, tiptoes across the floor in 6inch heels clutching a small gift. Entering the office, she perches on the edge of Mr Timms desk glancing only once out of the window to the faces looking back at her from the floor. This is it, 10am. The big announcement. 'Thank you for all coming here today', blah blah blah. It seems endless. Come on get to the point. 'So today is special'. Mr Timms stutter is not helping him. Did he just say Dunk? I'm sure he did. Oh no the biscuit underworld has been discovered, no more fun, no more wagers, Pug left on the shelf. He said it again Dunk! That's it, its over.

The blonde piece steps in to assist. 'Yes today marks 25 years service by Duncan Martin, and I'm pleased to give him his long service award'. Dunc the other kind steps forward, grinning and collects his 25 years' service commemorative plaque, to the sound of thunderous clapping. No one can actually believe anyone would sell toilet bowls for 25 years…

The room's awash with people returning to their workstations after the appropriate back patting of Dunc, who saved the day. Mr Timms and the blond piece who was later confirmed as his second wife, his first one left him for a plumber, waved goodbye to everyone. Sighs and phew were heard across the floor. Oops, Mr Timms is coming back he must have forgotten something I think. 'Geraldine' his voice whispers across my desk, 'Yes Mr Timms'. I glanced up trying not to look at his right eye that's a bit turned in… 'Tomorrow, at the break, will you put me £2 on a bourbon biscuit that lasts 45 seconds'.

Black Friday Bargains or not?

So the mad dash for buying Christmas presents begins, and everyone wants a bargain. Perhaps I'm imagining it, but the demands on parents seem to become higher each year. Children's expectations for this year's 'must have' toy ring in their parent's ears, assisted by the influx of social media coming from every angle. I fear for those who fall into debt whilst trying to keep up with the Jones's. My suggestion last year to the family was that everyone should spend only £10 on each other. This was not greeted with the joy that I thought it would be. I was trying to save them all some money, rather than discover four months later that the neatly wrapped present had never been used and was left loosely wrapped still in the bag or box, in a cupboard, or behind the settee. Does anyone need a foot spa, a box of designer soaps or a digital photo frame? I know where to find them.

I hadn't realised how predictable my choice of family Christmas presents was until my daughter pointed out that every year some of her presents are pretty much the same, pyjamas, slippers, 2 obligatory body sprays…etc. Maybe this year I'll get them all nothing, wonder if they'll predict that.

I do however like to get them a present that they can't guess. I'll wrap it in a way that disguises the contents and even a good squeeze reveals nothing. I once put, I think it was £20 for each of them, although it could have been £15, in 20p coins in a steradent tube. No one guessed what it was, but it was quite funny seeing the look on their faces as the wrapping paper unfolded to reveal a tube of Steradent Deep Cleaning Denture Tablets, or so they thought. This year I decided to do my Christmas shopping online, persuaded by the numerous adverts for Black Friday bargains, and the fact that it's cold outside, so here I sat at the computer with a steaming mug of hot chocolate, 2 choc chip cookies, my debit card, a cushion, and not a damn clue where to start. My immediate reaction is pyjamas; perhaps my daughter's right. Maybe I have a condition called Pyjamaitus, it's non-contagious and usually occurs in

November just after the flu jab season. I get it every year (apparently)! Wow, this is easy I think, as my shopping cart starts to fill up with what I believe to be the best bargains ever. I guess Black Friday is good after all. The cookies and hot chocolate are going down nicely and I'm working my way through the Christmas present list. I'm already fighting my Pyjamaitus; it's not easy though. I need a distraction for a minute as the withdrawal symptoms start, and the pull of buying cute, fluffy PJ'S draws me in, so I stop for a minute and refill my hot chocolate, this time without whipped cream and marshmallows. Browsing my list, I see a request from my youngest son. He's the hardest one to buy for. He likes unusual things, usually antique so I am always at a loss of what to get him, plus the fact that even the tiniest things are not usually cheap. His request for an antique watch is quickly discarded, as the cost does not fall into my price bracket. I pop his present into my online shopping basket and decide he might not have a clue what time it is, but at least he'll smell good. For some, I've opted for vouchers due to rising postal costs.

A few days later and all the lovely presents and vouchers arrive, some at the door, some I've missed, so a trudge to the sorting office is required and one parcel that was left by the courier in my dustbin, which in this instance I was grateful for. I have several reams of wrapping paper ready and a roll of sticky tape. I've forgotten to get any name labels, so this year should be fun for my son and daughter in law, as I needed to drop their presents off last week so I wrapped them up and left them without any labels on. It'll be more interesting on Christmas Day for them to see who unwraps what, and I can't see my son wearing age 4 Pink Unicorn pyjamas (my addiction got the better of me).

Today I sit here surrounded by all the lovely gift-wrapped presents and then I log onto Internet banking. I noticed my bank balance appears to have gone down quite significantly, much more than I anticipated. I start to look through all my Black Friday purchases, sale bargains I saw advertised. It is then, and only then, I realised its only Tuesday and I've paid full price….

Holidays are Coming...

So Christmas is almost upon us, and the Elf on the shelf has made his appearance. Where on earth did this tradition come from? I really like the idea that the children believe there's a mischievous elf looking over them, watching to see if they are naughty or nice. At least for parents, this probably means a few less tantrums over the next few weeks. It's a pity we didn't have one when I was a child. I could have blamed all the mischievous things on the elf that my sister usually did, and I got the blame for...

Here's a text message my daughter sent me this morning....

I was watching telly and Sienna (this is her daughter aged 4) disappeared into the kitchen. I can hear her crashing about, I said, 'Sienna what are you doing?' 'I'm making you some lunch mum; do you want a yoghurt for after?' She brings me a plate, some chunks of cheese,

3 wrinkly cherry tomatoes and some extra thick cucumber slices 'Here's your lunch, mum, I've got you a drink too'. (A whole cup of undiluted double strength blackcurrant) Sienna stands to watch me eat (I hid the tomatoes) 'Do you like it, mum?' 'Yes Sienna, it was delicious'. The elf watched me making your lunch, didn't he mum? He's going to tell Santa that I was good to you?

She brings me a yoghurt then says 'here mum have a drink.' I had a tiny sip. 'Thank you it's very strong, maybe it needs more water?' 'Mum, I made it strong just for you. Yes, that's fine.' I think I may need to borrow a child for the next few weeks.

Then there's the Christmas TV Advert competition between the rival supermarkets. Who'd have thought two carrots called Kevin & Katie could have such an impact. Have we gone completely barking mad? Our children now walk around cuddling and talking to carrots. Maybe they'll disappear after Christmas with seven sprouts and a stuffing ball. Christmas Day should be interesting with children all over the UK refusing to eat their carrots; after all, they couldn't eat poor Kevin, could they?

Years ago, I was asked if I would prepare a Christmas Lunch for 38 people. I actually ended up with 50 people as I felt the local brass band that offered free entertainment, on the day, should be fed as well. Having never cooked on this scale before, and with the words, 'never volunteer', ringing in my head, I agreed to do it, alongside 4 other 'volunteers'. Everything went extremely well, crackers were pulled and poppers popped as Christmas dinner was served. The only problem I encountered was my very large over-calculation of how many carrots I would need on the day. My solution to rid myself of this Kilimanjaro of carrots was for anyone, who didn't win a prize in our raffle, I gave them a booby prize.... Yes, a bag of carrots... It caused some disappointment, especially if you were hoping for a big box of chocs or a bottle of plonk. It caused great laughter too and a few strange looks as several people walked up the road at the same time swinging their little bag of what's now I suppose could be famously known as Kevin & Katie's. Onlookers, wondering why the hell, are all these people dressed up in their posh frocks or jackets walking up the road carrying carrots. I bet they were thinking I better get my carrots soon or there'll be none left...

The adverts are already enticing us, or tormenting us, if you are a parent. This year's must-have toy is apparently a doll named Luvabella, retailing at around £100, this is not cheap, but realistic, I kid you not. The only thing of concern for me is the doll's eyes, which are pretty freaky. Luvabella's a bit like Marmite; you either love it or hate it. I haven't decided yet....

Must dash...Now, what's that damn elf up to? arrgghh!!!!

The Office Christmas Party

It's the most wonderful time of the year. The office looks lovely for the Christmas party. Lots of tinsel and fairy lights, food spread out on a table in a corner and endless drink flowing, someone's already spilled some on the floor. Where's the wet floor sign? (Sorry Health & Safety moment).

Oh look, there's Mavis, she's usually dressed in a high-necked blouse and a straight skirt. Tonight she's wearing a racy little black number with sequin trim, even a tiny bit of cleavage was showing. She normally looks down her glasses, and peers over her computer with a don't-ask-me sort of expression. But here she is tonight; two white wines and twirling around on the dance floor like a launched spinning top apologising as she goes, in the arms of Geoff. Fifteen years her senior, Geoff's quite a twinkle toes on the dance floor. He's wearing his Rudolph Christmas jumper and well-polished brown shoes. Like Fred Astaire and Ginger Rogers, they stop for no one, devouring the dance floor with their sweeping moves. Mavis giggling is totally out of character. Geoff reaches occasionally for his pint of real ale and licks his lips.

Glancing to my left I see Amy. Amy's miserable as sin, if sin could be miserable that is it, has no one told her it's a party. I think Dave might be telling her now. New starter, Dave, he's only been here for a fortnight but already knows where the toilet is, and how long he can stretch it out for. Often disappears for long periods, sadly not many people notice. Looks like he's asking Amy to dance. Oh, she's declined, probably doesn't want to get caught up in the washing machine that's Mavis & Geoff. Oh, Dave's trying again. Give up Dave it's not going to happen. Oh, Amy's moving looks like she may have changed her mind. Oh no, she's spotted the mushroom vol au vents being carried through and is following them, nose to the ground like a bloodhound. No weight watchers weigh in this week then. Poor Dave, all deflated. I can see he's making a mental note to try again later. Change of tempo, the music stops, and time for the Annual Appreciation speech, prize giving and certificate presentation. Here goes...lights come on, spotlight on Mr Williamson (George Williamson, Office Manager ...You can call me George, but ONLY for tonight). On all other occasions, you can lick my boots and kiss my arse. First to get his certificate is Billy, the best one-armed cleaner I've ever known, actually the only one-armed cleaner I've ever known. Now, Joan, I knew she'd get one. I often work late, tucked away and unseen in my little workspace. I've heard the moans and groans from the photocopy room and have seen the light flicking on and off under the door. George entering and leaving quite regularly with a smug expression on his face and Joan leaving without any paperwork, both looking like someone turned the heating up, funny that...I wonder what it says on her certificate ' Proficient use of photocopier' Anyway he's given it to her now. She smiles as she leaves the stage. Did you see that? George checking out her butt whilst everyone claps...

Denise enters the room. Bold as brass, that one, she's already winched Geoff away from Mavis and she's trying to manoeuvre his body under the mistletoe. I can see he's digging his heels in, but with that well-buffed floor, resistance is futile, as he slips until he is appropriately positioned and Denise proceeds to disengage his tonsils. Poor Mavis looks on bewildered. The clapping on stage continues as Geoff eventually emerges, dishevelled, wondering what day it is.

I think that may be the end of the Certificates of Appreciation. 'Oh no', I think I heard my name, 'I did'. Why would I get a certificate, all I did all year was take the pi** out of everyone. I suppose I did save the finger of the young lady, whose accident in the elevator saw the end of her finger going up and down until I rescued it, and the local hospital glued it back on. 'Oh well here goes', up the steps I go, shake hands with George, mandatory turn to the camera, smile at onlookers and accept my Certificate of Appreciation, alongside a free copy of hospital news and a years supply of sticky plasters. I bet Joan got wet wipes…

Knock, knock, knocking...

I'm standing in a very long queue. I can see people for miles in front of me. Looking around, there's no one in this queue I recognise. I chat to the person next to me, and we continuing walking. On the journey, we become good friends and we laugh as we continue to walk.In the far distance I can see a sign, but I can't quite read it. I can see the queue further up starting to split and I can see two directional arrows, one pointing to two huge gates straight ahead of me, the other points to a sign, which says 'This way for elevator'. The crowd only moves in one direction. 'Sorry mate', there's no going back now, I hear someone say.

I arrive at the front of the queue and the man with the clipboard stops me. He searches frantically for my name on his long list, unravelling as he goes. The gates are open, but not wide enough for me to get through. I try to peek inside, but Peter, the man with the clipboard won't let me. Next thing, Peter calls his colleague over, 'this ones not on the list'. 'We've got one of them inbetweenies' he says. 'Ok, take him down for interrogation. I've looked at his file', he says, pulling out a USB stick. 'His conduct on earth has been somewhat inconclusive'. What does he mean? I suddenly realise that the sign I was looking at are the gates of heaven or hell. I'm led away and taken to a large training room. Several other people are waiting. We sit and a DVD comes on, called, 'All about you'. It's about good and bad. 'Yes, I'm getting out of here soon', I think.. I'll be going through those heavenly gates singing,' 'Heaven must be missing an Angel'. Five more minutes and they'll be measuring me up for my halo. 'Coffee and chocolate biscuits and then comes the written test', Peter says.

During the break, I look around the room. I see a large clock and a glass elevator with people inside. It goes down continuously, slowly past the only window in the room. I never see it come back up again. There is an occasional warm orange glow rising from the bottom of the glass and someone in our room burns their fingertips as they touch the inside of the window. Someone quickly administers first aid and they are ushered back to their seat.

'Ok, your written exam is about to start. You have 30 minutes. You must answer all the questions, no talking is allowed and once you have finished raise your hand.'

'Begin', Peter says.... I look at the paper and think, this is easy...

Have you ever lied about something?

Answer: No

Have you ever taken something that didn't belong to you?

Answer: No

Have you ever wished something bad would happen to someone?

Answer: No

Three minutes later. I look around everyone else is frantically scribbling away.... I raise my hand. Are you finished? I'm asked. 'Yes', I say.... He looks at my paper, shakes his head, mutters something about denial and produces a USB stick out of his pocket...

Question 1) Have you ever lied about something?

Answer: No

Really? 'What about the time you recently went shopping with your friend and she asked if her dress looked good on her, and you said yes, well it didn't, did it'?

Or the time you were asked 'who put the chewing gum on the teacher's chair'? You denied all knowledge whilst clutching the packet in your pocket...

Question 2)

Have you ever taken something that didn't belong to you? Answer: No

'Remember the time you took a penny out of your mother's purse, to buy sweets with'. 'But I was six at the time'. I try to reason to no avail...

Question 3) Have you ever wished something bad would happen to someone? Answer: No

What about the time.. 'Ok', I've had enough by now. I feel like a deer caught in the headlights and my halo slipping. 'Take him down', Peter says.

I stood, waiting for the elevator to take me down. I can feel the heat as it rises, see the glowing embers below and hear screaming noises in the distance.

All at once, I feel a tugging and hear a familiar ringing noise. In a daze, I open my eyes and find myself wrapped like a mummy in my duvet, my alarm clock ringing in my ears. I jump quickly out of bed and got ready for work.

Today is going to be a good day. Would I lie to you?…..

Peed off and Seagulls

I was wondering what sort off things irritate you; for me like anyone there's the usual stuff like leaving the toilet seat up and the top off the toothpaste, others include:

- Uneven table legs

- Peeled beer mats

- Standing in dog poo, especially if you're on your way to a job interview

- Mr or Mrs Right

- The hypochondriac who explains everything in graphic detail

- People using phones at the dining table

This week I thought I'd try out my new Camper van awning. Arriving at the Campsite I unravelled this huge beast of an awning. It was so big; I could barely lift it off the van seat, as I did it landed on the floor with a thud like a missile. I was feeling pretty pleased with myself as I checked off my list, awning (tick), pegs (tick), pump (tick). I'd watched a five-minute master class on awning erection on YouTube in preparation, so I felt adequately knowledgeable. What I wasn't prepared for was a faulty pump, one that blew air out but then sucked it back in again. After several attempts to rectify the problem I gave up. A trip to the local shop to buy an electric pump was fruitless and I came out carrying 4 pints of semi skimmed milk and three bananas, neither of which I really needed.

It seems this was the start of a night of problems. Firstly the van radio became erratic and was flickering on/off but without any sound, the TV, phone and Internet had no reception. The electric hook cable up failed to provide electric and the Leisure battery died. I spent a night in candlelight, wrapped up like someone going to the North Pole. This was unplanned wild camping at its best and I was traumatised by my lack of Internet.

The following morning I decided to try out the shower block. I'm not saying it was far away, but hiking boots and a compass would have been useful. Anyway, it's 8am I'm stood naked in the shower, when I heard an almighty bang directly above my head. I almost feared to look up, but I did. The roof above my head was made of almost clear corrugated plastic and standing directly above me was a Seagull. If you've ever wondered, probably not, what the underneath of a seagulls webbed feet look like, well this was the view I had. It was actually quite fascinating, yes, I know I need to get out more. The seagull didn't stick around long, probably because of the view he had looking down.

Sadly I think all the excitement finally got too much for my beloved Camper van 'Trixie'. She was last seen on the back of a tow truck waiting for a mechanic to revive her. The lack of available early morning taxis to work however as spurred me on to getting my pushbike out of the garage. You will remember my last experience, was when the man on the mobility scooter overtook me, laughing. Knowing nothing about bikes I have now discovered that my bike was in sixth gear and had deflated tyres. It's hardly surprising that I was almost in cardiac arrest last time out. I don't think I'll be doing the Tour De France this year, but who knows…

Jeff the stand-in Best Man

Have you ever been to a wedding and listened to the best man's speech. Here's one I prepared earlier, I hope you like it.

'I thought I'd start my speech today with the usual thank you to everyone for coming. To the bridesmaids, the wedding planner and the guests, especially those bearing gifts, although, judging by the boxes, we already have three toasters and two ironing boards.

For those of you who don't know me, it's always good to arrive early at weddings. If you don't like the look of the person you're sitting next to, you can always swop the place names before anyone else gets seated. Remember that you can't all avoid Auntie Mary.

Today, we're here to celebrate the wedding of Christopher and his new wife, Sally. I wonder, how long it takes for a new wife to become an old one. Anyway, what can I say about Christopher? I can tell, he'll make a wonderful husband. I can see some of you nodding already. A great father. Oops, hope I didn't let the cat out of the bag. And judging by the size of his Ferrari, I can say he's doing very well.

Before I forget. Have you seen the wedding cake? I've never seen one like it before. Four layers of cheese & pork pie. I wondered why there was a bowl of pickle next to it. It's okay until you get to the Stilton. Can't stand the stuff myself. Maybe they could try fruitcake next time.

Actually, I have a confession to make. Christopher and Sally are friends with my identical twin brother Kevin. For those of you who don't know, the real best man, Jonathon, lies in hospital following an unfortunate encounter with a ski lift in the Pyrenees. 'Christopher, then asked Kevin my identical twin to stand in for him.

Unfortunately last night after the stag do, at around midnight, driven by an insane desire for chocolate, Kevin decided to go for a walk, looking for a shop. He was heavily intoxicated, and when offered a lift home by a driver, he readily accepted. He gave the driver his address and told him he was going to a wedding in the morning. The driver suggested he sleep his hangover off'. 'Early this morning, I received a phone call from his pregnant wife, 350 miles away, asking me why he was home, and was the wedding off? Luckily, I happened to be working in the area.

Without further adieu, please raise your glasses to the bride and groom, Christopher and Sally, absent friends and the chef. The Pavlova is to die for. My name is Jeff, the stand in Best Man'.

Morning as broken

This is the second morning I've been woken up by the postman ringing my doorbell. I run excitedly, ok, so maybe not run, downstairs in my pj's, hair looking like I've just removed my finger from an electric socket. My fingers are twitching in anticipation of signing for some surprise parcel. What does the postman say as I open the door, 'Sorry, I pushed the wrong post through'. I'm quite a patient person, but this is twice now in the same week. I've decided if it happens again, I'm not answering the door. Although, if I don't I may end up missing out on a parcel myself and have to go and collect it from the sorting office. I suppose I could peep out of the upstairs window, and see what he's carrying.

I'm not sure about mornings. People say 'oh, I'm a morning person or I'm a night owl'. I'm used to getting up at 5am for my 6.30am start at work, but I can't say I enjoy it, except on days off, when the sun is shining and then I'm happy to be up early.

I'm definitely, not a night owl though; I find it hard to keep awake on any day after 10pm. When me and my sister go on holiday, we try to do this once a year, no men, no children, just us, by 10pm we are usually sat up in bed watching some German film with subtitles,on one occasion the subtitles were missing. It was the only channel we could tune into at the time. We watched the film right to the very end or at least I did. It was quite interesting, partly because you could sort of tell from the pictures what was going on, the rest I made up with my vivid imagination. Let's just say it was interesting...

I remember years ago, being woken up as a child by the familiar sound of the milkman, delivering bottles of milk to your doorstep at about five o'clock in the morning. These days even the birds seem to have a lie in until later. I suppose there's no point for them getting up so early now, with no milk bottle lids to peck on. What I really like is waking up to the sound of the waves crashing on the beach and the smell of the sea air. Living on a main road on the edge of a town offers neither of these, although usually the idiot on the motorbike, honking his horn obliges with his early morning wake up call.

I really do need to get a new blind for my kitchen window. I've just seen a rare double decker bus driving past, and saw people looking in at me, on my bad hair day.

So you've grabbed your breakfast, the healthy option of course, methodically blended fruit, oats and yoghurt, watched a bit of TV, assuming it's your day off and you've nothing better to do, what next? Why not try a little 'tachi yomi', it sounds like a form of exercise I know, but its not. It actually means 'standing reading'. In the UK if we go into a supermarket or bookshop and stand there reading the magazines for ages, sooner or later someone will pass a comment about 'if you're not buying that, do you mind putting it down'. In Japan 'tachi yomi is often welcomed. People stand for hours reading their favourite magazines in convenience stores. This is seen to encourage more people to come into the store. I wonder if they actually buy any though?

Maybe I should try it next time I go to the supermarket. I'll pick up my favourite magazine, if anyone asks what I'm doing I'll just reply 'tachi yomi', and say nothing else. They may think I don't understand and ignore me, alternatively they may call the security guard and have me escorted off the premises, knowing me it'll be the latter. I can see my face in the local paper now and the headlines 'Woman declares Tachi Yomi' whilst clutching tightly onto magazine in local supermarket...

Once Upon A Time

Once upon at time, there was a young woman who left school at sixteen, with dreams of being an English Teacher; somehow those dreams got left behind. Married at 18 and caught up in the daily grind of life, she worked hard to pay her bills, feed and clothe her children, and keep a roof over their heads.

Many years later in her fifties she found herself alone. She'd never written since leaving school but inspired by a close friend, she put pen to paper for the first time and in 2016 the journey began.

In 2017 with the help of her daughter she set up a Facebook page Battenberg & Banter and started posting weekly blogs, and with the continued support of her friend she decided to write a book. She wanted one that would make people smile, laugh and cry all at the same time. A book of escapism, realism and courage to live life without regret. That woman is I.

Follow your dreams, if I can do it, so can you!

The End

Thank you

I would like to thank the following people for their thoughts, ideas, friendship, inspiration, help and support during the creation and publication of this book, without them I wouldn't be sane, that's if I still am? Please let this book be an inspiration to others to show them that anything is possible….

Sincere thanks go to -

My family

First born

Artur The bat (May you RIP)

Brian 'You know who you are'

References

Divorce is on the rise among over 50's in the UK. Just retirement Ltd. 7/2/2018

How Many Calories Do You Burn Each Time You Laugh? Livestrong Article 308619 18/7/17

Rats laugh when tickled – and this is what it sounds like. Telegraph, Adam Boult

Indy/Eats The best biscuit for dunking in tea revealed. The Independent Rachel Hosie 18/4/2018

'The funniest toilet jokes ever told'

Splash Direct 12/12/13

Holly Willoughby – Interview with worlds largest dog This Morning news Digital spy

84 Amazing facts about spiders Fact Retriever, https://www.factretriever.com/spider-facts

Karin Lehnardt, Senior Writer, August 21, 2016

Mother-of-two fed up of waiting for late buses invoices company for her wasted time - and wins

Daily Mail news article 29330008 30/1/2015

10 things you may not know about laughter
https://articles.mercola.com/sites/articles/archive/2014/11/13/10-fascinating-facts-laughter.aspx

Why do people put candles on birthday cakes

https://www.google.co.uk/search?rlz=1C1CHFX_enGB497GB497&q=Why+do+people+put+candles+on+birthday+cakes%3F&sa=X&ved=2ahUKEwjUmOjBip_dAhWpDMAKHc48DxAQzmd6BAgFEAk&biw=1024&bih=662

Stop Jet Ski Accidents in their wake
https://www.tariolaw.com/stop_jet_ski_accidents_in_their_wake_/

Printed in Poland
by Amazon Fulfillment
Poland Sp. z o.o., Wrocław